THE BRIDE OF
AMMAN

Praise for *The Bride of Amman*:

Think *Sex and the Citadel* meets Ramadan soap: *The Bride of Amman* is a dramatic portrait of young men and women looking for love in a time of taboo. An insightful and impassioned account of the high cost of social conformity—in and out of the bedroom.

> - Shereen El Feki, author of *Sex and the Citadel: Intimate Life in a Changing Arab World*

Fadi Zaghmout engages the full range of human emotion as he confronts head-on the destructive, corrosive effects of prejudice, tradition, and male privilege on sexuality, sexual expression, and gender identity. Charged, dynamic, and engaging, *The Bride of Amman* is sure to disturb and please—and to remain with readers long after they've finished Zaghmout's compelling narrative of four lives desperate for liberation.

> - Matthew Weinart, Associate Professor and Director of Graduate Studies, Political Science & International Relations Department, University of Delaware

In this book, Fadi Zaghmout beautifully criticizes the values of the Arab society, smoothly switches between ridiculing our most sacred traditions and exposing the devastating effects that they can have on our lives. We laugh and we cry, but at the end we can't but feel comforted that he managed to express what we all think and feel, ourselves.

> - George Azzi, gender and sexual rights activist,
> co-founder of AFE and Helem

A powerful narrative, an intricate braid of secrets, exposing Jordanian society's hypocrisy and obsession with the institution of marriage. Its pioneering feminist vision is a bid for tolerance, equality, and freedom. A compulsive read.

> - Fadia Faqir, author of
> *Willow Trees Don't Weep*

The Bride of Amman is unputdownable and a rattlingly significant read. Fadi Zaghmout creates a wonderfully distinctive polyphonic narrative of the characters' selves trying to engage with the world around them to act or to make choices. While the novel voices the marginalization and disempowerment of its characters struggling to fit in a culturally conditioned and constructed subjective identity, it neatly weaves the narrative of its characters negotiating an active role within society's power dynamics. A must-read novel to understand how subjective identity and culture shape one another.

> - Wafa Alkhadra, Professor at American
> University of Madaba, Jordan

In *The Bride of Amman*, Fadi Zaghmout has written what I consider is one of the first Jordanian novels to challenge the taboos of gender exploration. Incredibly and skilfully, he manages to move us across that invisible line without anger, challenge, attitude, or negativity. He holds our hand and softly encourages us to explore new worlds within our familiar surroundings. A must read!

> - Nermeen Murad, Chief of Party of USAID Takamol Gender Program; writer, columnist, gender-, and human-rights advocate

It is a brave book that weaves together lives that are in conflict with the *diktats* of religious, patriarchal, and societal mores—the three hegemonies that submerge and suffocate truthful expressions of gender and sexuality. The personal accounts are chilling, and I find a lot of resonance with similar issues faced by women and gay men in India. The book also offers hope that challenges can be overcome and life can be lived on one's own terms within the matrix of our societies. The simplicity of the truthful writing, and the complexity of the emotions the characters undergo, takes the reader on a roller-coaster journey that is thought-provoking and invigorating. More power to Fadi and the book, and for empowerment of women and the LGBT community, world-over.

> - Sridhar Rangayan, filmmaker and activist, Mumbai, India

The Bride of Amman evoked in my heart a longing for freedom. A bold and painful novel, it tells the stories of women I recognise, and I can see myself in them—I could have been one of them.

> - Saba Mubarak, Jordanian actress and producer

Gender, sex, and sexuality: the unspoken issues in Arab societies are addressed creatively and sensitively in a novel that embraces all walks of life. Every Arab woman should read this book to gain more insight into empowerment of gender, feminism, and sexuality. Every Arab man should read this book to get a glimpse of what Arab women endure under male domination—and how their mothers, sisters, and homosexual brothers have had it tough.

- Madian Al Jazerah, owner of books@cafe,
Amman, Jordan

THE BRIDE OF AMMAN

A novel by

FADI ZAGHMOUT
Translated from the Arabic
by Ruth Ahmedzai Kemp

Signal 8 Press
Hong Kong

The Bride of Amman
By Fadi Zaghmout
Published by Signal 8 Press
An imprint of Typhoon Media Ltd
Copyright 2012 Fadi Zaghmout
English translation copyright 2015 Ruth Ahmedzai
Kemp
ISBN: 978-988-12198-9-3
eISBN: 978-988-12198-2-4

Typhoon Media Ltd:
Signal 8 Press | Distribution | Consultancy
Hong Kong
www.typhoon-media.com

First published in Arabic under the title *Aroos Amman*
in 2012 by Jabal Amman Publishers (Amman, Jordan).

Cover image: Madalena Ng (Protein Creative)
Author photo: Mohammed Al Nabulsi

Contents

Author's dedication:

To Arab young men and women: those who are struggling to conform, those who are fighting for autonomy over their own bodies, and those advocating for sexual rights

Translator's dedication:

For Norm, for all your love and support

PART ONE

LEILA

No bride without a groom

WHAT a day! I've been battered by wave after wave of conflicting emotions: proud, optimistic smiles; tears of frustration and despair. I'm sprawled out on my bed, numb, adrift in the thoughts whirling round my head. I try to grasp hold of something, to make sense of where I am.

Life can be so strange, and tears and smiles are twin sisters who are never far apart. For all their differences, they seem to particularly like showing up at the same party.

I got up early this morning. Sleep eluded me last night; I barely shut an eyelid. My thoughts were all focused on that piece of paper that represents the keys to my future—or so I thought. A small white sheet of paper listing the results of four years of my life at university and the long nights spent surrounded by equations and numbers, dreams of success and of fulfilling the ambition I've had since I was a child.

I partly have Loai to thank for my success, the know-it-all in my class whose marks I have always kept an eye on, making sure I did better. He's been a great source of motivation, and his being male made me even more determined to beat him. It was him who made me realise the sheer scale of the sexual discrimination I faced, when he told me his father's reaction once after I got a higher score than him in class.

"Shame on you! Being floored by a girl!"

His father's sarcastic taunt has rung in my ears ever since, like a blast of dynamite propelling me to beat them all and knock Loai, his dad, and all of their sex to the floor. Yes, I'm a woman and yes, I have passed my degree with a distinction. That's what I want to be recognised for.

It was such a proud feeling to see my name atop the list of those awarded a distinction, and my mood couldn't be tainted even by Lana. I did my best to ignore her patronising look as she waved her hand in my face, trying to make her gesture seem completely normal, while making sure I couldn't fail to spot the ring on her finger. I could hardly miss it, but I pretended not to notice. She kept on waving it about, congratulating me with a smile through gritted teeth. Yet she was obviously quite confident about the superiority of her success: of course, getting engaged is, in her eyes but also in everyone else's, a much more significant achievement than getting a degree.

"Omar and I are getting married," she said, nauseatingly draping herself over his shoulder.

She lost patience with my underwhelmed response and thrust the ring at my face. I found myself having to force a smile and recognise, against my will, her 'graduation' to this superior level of existence. I extended my arms to give her a hug, aware of how unconvincing my facial expression must be. After much effort, and what seemed like an eternity, I finally managed to force out an ice-cold response.

"Congratulations."

Omar was the first man in my life. I met him in my early days at university. He liked me and chased after me quite persistently for a while. I liked him too, but I turned him down. I didn't have the self-confidence to know how to behave around men I didn't know. I'm from a single-sex school and a conservative family that prohibits any kind of romance before marriage. My firm principles didn't help me control my feelings, though. I still liked him. And I crumbled in the face of his persistence and eventually started meeting up with him under very strict conditions—which I imposed. But these suffocating restrictions left our relationship with no room to breathe: no exchanging gifts, no calling me after college, no seeing each other after college… no, no, no—nothing was allowed!

Omar left me after three months. Just after I'd really fallen for him. Fallen in love for the first time in my life. He had no time for all the rules I imposed on him. His interest in me fizzled out just when he had captured my heart and soul. I was willing to compromise on some of my principles and perhaps accept a few of his, but he didn't give me the chance.

The tears welled up in my eyes when he told me that he had decided to end our relationship. I tried to suppress my emotions, but I failed. My dignity held me back from arguing or asking why.

"Is this your final decision?" I asked.

He nodded. I bent my head down and left without saying a word.

I simply couldn't give him any more. Lana, on the other hand, is different: she's from another community, a completely different background. She sees herself as liberal, whereas in our eyes she's just shameless. She can't speak without flirting, doing everything she can to flaunt her charms. Men flock around her, while all the girls steer clear of her. Many people would say she's beautiful, but I can't see it myself. Perhaps it's because her unpleasant personality makes her seem ugly to me, or perhaps it's just jealousy. Either way, it isn't a fair contest.

Rana and Hayat agree with me. We call her 'Barbie' and the three of us are always trying to outdo each other in our impersonations of her. Today we were all standing there together at the entrance to the Business faculty. As always, I was watching Lana and Omar, while Rana couldn't keep her eyes off Janty, and Hayat was gazing at all the other men in the faculty. 'The terrible trio,' we were brought together by university life and by our common hatred of Lana. Rana is the most outgoing: she's definitely got the gift of gab. Hayat is quite a private person: she doesn't give a lot away, but she's always very sharp and astute. And as for me—I tend to play by the book. I guess you could say I'm the serious one.

On any other day, Lana acting like that would really irritate me and put me in a foul mood. But today was different. I had just got my degree results—a distinction!—and I couldn't wait to tell my family and see the proud look in their eyes. Of course, my mother expected nothing less. She also got up really early this morning and had already invited her friends and our neighbors and relatives over to celebrate my results day with us.

When I walked into the house, I was greeted like a bride, with the shrill sound of the women's squeals and ululations. I was proud of myself and what I'd achieved, and was over-joyed that so many of our female friends and family had come to celebrate with me. My mother's trill was especially ear-splitting. She hugged me, squeezing me tight.

"And may a husband be soon to follow," she said softly in my ear. My mum moved on, leaving me to my aunt's embrace.

"And soon, I hope, we'll see you in your own home," whispered my aunt.

My eyes roamed from one beaming face to another as I heard everyone whisper their wishes to me in turn.

"*Mashallah*, you'll be a bride soon. It's God's will."

"*Inshallah*, God willing, we'll see you married and happy."

"God willing, you'll be as clever when it comes to cooking."

I turned to look at my older sister Salma. She was sitting next to my grandmother, silent and distracted, while the other women were chattering away, reeling off their prolific wish lists for my future. My grandmother was also silent for a long time, until a curse spilled from her lips.

"I should know, for God's sake. I got married at 14," she suddenly muttered, shaking her head. "We used to get married young, not like these days... *Yallah*... God help us, don't end up like your sister. No one wants to be an unplucked fruit left to rot."

Salma turned pale, stunned by this slap in the face. I watched her as she tried to hold back her tears. She couldn't.

She was obviously embarrassed, and dashed off to our room. I tried to catch up with her to console her, but stopped when I heard the girls' shrieks and ululations start up again.

"What?" I asked, rushing back to where the noise was coming from. The answer came from my cousin Hiba.

"I'm pregnant!"

Most of the women swarmed around her as though she were the one the party was intended for. I was no longer the *aroos*, the bride, the star of the party: there's no bride without a groom, after all. This reality struck me that moment like a bolt of lightning. All those years I'd wasted trying to prove myself. I genuinely believed that getting a degree would raise my value in everyone's eyes and establish my status as a fully independent woman. But at that moment I was stopped in my tracks, thunderstruck, by the realisation that my degree was in fact nothing more than another step on the path towards the ultimate goal: marriage.

SALMA

Thirty—the dreaded expiry date

MY eyes roam across the ceiling of the room which has cradled Leila and me since our earliest childhood. I look across at her and see she's fast asleep, all signs of distress erased from her tanned face. She had her hair done for the party and now a lock of her chestnut brown hair has unravelled and falls across her rosy cheek.

I sigh and get up from my bed. I go over to Leila and gently place a kiss on her forehead.

"I'm sorry," I whisper.

The pain chokes me, like I'm being strangled. My grandmother's words earlier were like a scalpel that sliced through my mask of self-confidence, the defences I'd built around me for the occasion. I'd steeled myself for being put on the spot and for the usual embarrassing questions, and even the odd provocative comment, and yet I crumbled because of one stray bullet that shot out of my grandmother's mouth.

I couldn't hold back the tears and ran away to hide in my room. I was furious with myself and even more so with her. I scolded myself not just for being weak, but also for being selfish. How could I forget that today was Leila's happy day? How could I wallow in my own misfortune and ruin my sister's party with my foul mood? What right did I have to dwell on my despair about the future on the very day when she was so excited about hers?

When I saw the look on her face, I realised that the bullet my grandmother had shot was ringing in her ears, too. Her eyes were suddenly forced open to the scenario I'm stuck in: the fear that starts to spread like an ulcer through the mind of a girl at Leila's age.

"An unplucked fruit left to rot."

How could my grandmother say such a vile thing? To reduce us both to a piece of fruit that no one wants to taste. Thirty—the dreaded expiry date. I associate it with death: it's the first time a girl dies in a society that can't wait to write its daughters off as 'old maids.' Ugh, that word makes me shudder!

The countdown begins as soon as you graduate—sometimes even before. It's a race against the clock, a marathon of a race, where every woman is scrambling to the front to bag herself a husband. You have to use your female wiles in this survival of the fittest, where survival means being lucky enough to be snapped up. But the door to the other side gradually creaks shut as the clock ticks towards the age of thirty, when you are written off as surplus goods, marked down as a social failure, and condemned to a marginal role on the fringes of society.

Sometimes I try to shut my eyes and ignore the dreaded number, but everyone seems to insist on reminding me. The latest was Mona, a good friend of mine who finished the 'marathon' last year at the grand old age of twenty-nine. She had no shame about sighing with relief in front of me.

"*Alhamdu lillah! Alhamdu lillah!* Thank God, I managed to get married before I was thirty!"

Honestly, the cheek of it. As if fortune had saved her from some near-fatal disaster. Utter disregard for the fact that I am on the verge of turning thirty with no fiancé in sight.

I have never been one of 'the fittest.' Being one of the 'fittest' in this contest, to most people, equates to physical beauty. I try to seem confident and happy with my looks, but basically I'm putting on an act, playing up my strong, loveable personality to make up for what I lack in looks. I have to be cheerful and funny to compensate, but, inside, I am fragile. My heart is delicate, like glass that shatters into tiny shards, lacerating me at the slightest comment about my appearance or the slightest hint of a comparison between me and another woman in terms of my looks. I try to dismiss other women who obsess about being attractive as vacuous and stupid, and I'm always the first to crack jokes about women like that. I was the one who coined the name 'Barbie' for Lana, Leila's classmate at uni. Of course, Leila was in stitches when I started that. From then on, whenever I meet the 'terrible trio,' they always want me to do my impersonation of her. I get out a bright red lipstick and paint my lips and cheeks, all gaudy and completely over the top. I unbutton my shirt to reveal a little cleavage, tilt my head and pout. It's never long before Leila, Rana, and Hayat are rolling about in laughter as I strut around, flaunting my curves and fluttering my eyelashes.

"Omarrrr..." I purr, in a soft, velvety voice. "Do you love me?"

Rana nods, taking the part of Omar. I twirl my hair flirtatiously in my fingers, plait it and put it in my mouth. I wiggle my bum and mince about all coquettishly, until I fall flat on the floor and all four of us are in fits of hysterical giggles.

***

I fetch the laptop and sit down on my bed, casting a glance at the picture of my nephew on my bedside table. I give him a quick kiss, then put it back. I open up my blog, *The Jordanian Spinster*, which I began last year under this pseudonym. I started it because I want to communicate with people, and talk about my fears and my dreams, and about the great expectations placed on my shoulders as a Jordanian woman in a society that is full of pressures and obligations. Most of all I write about the obsession Jordanian women have with marriage. What is it that makes us behave in such a maniacal way, often against all logic and reason?

A few days ago, I was thinking about Ali, my nephew who I'm besotted with. My brother Mohammed got married two years ago when he was twenty-five. It was barely a couple of months after the wedding before his wife was pregnant. Ali arrived nine months later, and since that day he's been a source of utter joy for the whole family, and for me in particular. I have developed this incredibly strong attachment to him, and he's one of the few things in my life that still puts a smile on my face.

But my love for gorgeous little Ali hasn't distracted me from worrying about myself and my future. I know that time is flying by at lightning speed. My biological clock is ticking away furiously, while as far as my social clock is concerned, time has basically already stopped.

"Will fortune ever smile on me?" I write in my blog.

Will I ever be a mother myself one day? My anxiety grows the older I get. The years hurtle by, as oblivious and merciless as a train speeding over the frail body of a child. With each year that passes, my pain escalates and I avoid celebrating my birthday. I switch off my mobile and shut myself up in my room for the day.

Struggling with this anxiety, I construct another world for myself, immersed in my imagination. I see myself carrying a tiny baby, a little girl I've named Yasmine. Her smell is like the scent of sweet jasmine nectar. I hold her close to my chest and shut my eyes. I fill this imaginary world with moments of indescribable joy, all crafted to erase my unhappy reality.

Where does this obsession with children come from anyway? Is it an inevitable outcome that nature imposes on us women? Or is it a reflection of our social upbringing, the reality of our environment that forces our thoughts in this direction? Is it a selfish need that arises from our fear of death and our desire for a successor to inherit our genes? Or does it stem from the effusive energy that emanates from a woman's heart, a source of compassion that needs a receptacle to pour into? Is it an innate role she is predestined to assume to complete the cycle of life?

I sigh, and continue writing.

Who can I blame in this world for making my whole life

revolve around a man who is notable only by his absence?
Do I curse Cinderella? Or Snow White? Should I despise
Shakespeare for planting the seed of Romeo and Juliet in my
imagination? Or is it perhaps all my schoolteacher's fault
for filling my mind with romantic poetry, such as the story
of Leila and Majnun, of Qais's undying love for Leila? Or
maybe the poet Jamil ibn Ma'mar is to blame with his eulo-
gies of chaste love for Buthaynah, honouring his passion
which would never and could never be fulfilled.

I delete the last paragraph and then click the 'post' button. I wait a while, then reload the page. I check the number of comments in the hope that someone might have already read it and written something in response. I find the number is zero, so open my emails to kill some time. A few minutes later I leave my email and open my blog page again. The number has changed to one, so I open the comments. There is one posted by someone with the user name Yasmine:

How I have dreamed of a mother to hold me tight and show
me that tenderness you describe in a woman's love for a
baby she has not yet given birth to. Because, dear friend, I
lost my mother when I was a young child and I grew up
trying to picture how she would look, and imagine the love
and affection she would lavish on me. As time went by, my
mother's image has changed in my mind's eye, but my longing
for her loving embrace has never diminished with the years,
and since I got married and had children myself, I, too, as a
mother have been elated to smell that sweet nectar scent on
my sons and daughters.

If I could turn back time, I would run into your arms, desperate to feel the comfort of your love and affection. I'd throw my arms around you as the mother whom I have never known except in my imagination. I have always wondered what goes through my mother's mind: has she forgotten me? Does she miss me? Would she recognise me? Does she see me out and about as she goes about her life? Do I pop up in her daydreams like she does in mine?

Today is the first time I've had an answer to my questions, as if God Almighty gave her a way to send me a message through you. In her world, she has indeed always been holding me close and breathing in my sweet nectar scent. Now, at last, I can relax, reassured. So thank you, Mum. I love you, too, and I am so excited about finally meeting you one day.

And you, dear friend, I'm sure your little girl Yasmine is just as excited about meeting you one day, too.

Please, for your sake and hers, I hope that day will be soon.

Thank you,
Yasmine

Wow. I am completely bowled over by Yasmine's words! For a moment I genuinely feel we are mother and daughter. That we are one single entity, bound together by an invisible thread which fate wrenched from us and threw away into the depths of time. I can't help wondering if there really is a hidden link between us.

Is it insane to imagine that we could really have been a mother and daughter in another life and another era? Or that maybe we still will be some day in another life to come? Might fate somehow intervene in bringing Yasmine's life to an end, thus passing her soul to the child I may one day have?!

I shudder, quickly trying to shake this disturbing idea. Have I completely lost my mind, to the extent that I might rejoice, even for a moment, in the idea of another person dying? How can I possibly allow such selfish instincts to rampage through my mind without even being aware of it?

I desperately need a cigarette. I get up to open my bedroom window and close the door. I rummage around for the packet amongst all the make-up and stuff in my handbag. I take out a cigarette and light it, standing next to the window, on guard in case my father enters suddenly. My eyes catch sight of the picture of the tattered lungs on the packet and, unconsciously, I read the warning, 'Smoking kills.'

I take a deep drag and then another, and another. I finish the cigarette and go back to bed. I try to sleep but I can't. My mind is spinning with Yasmine's words and my grandmother's. There are moments when I feel certain that I'll never get married, and I feel like I'm having a panic attack. My heart starts racing and I can't catch my breath.

I close my eyes again and hold Yasmine tight to my chest. A stranger's arms reach out and take her from me.

"Yasmine!" I scream, as I see her drifting further and further away from me. I scream and scream, and I open my eyes. I get up, light another cigarette, then a second and a third, and so on until the early hours of the morning.

HAYAT

Why do I always fall for such losers?

IT took a while for my boss's words to sink in. She was sacking me from my job in her dressmaking sweatshop and she was saying it with the same mix of patronising bluntness and disdain that I'd got used to over the past few months.

"I don't employ filthy girls!" she said, looking down her nose at me. "The reputation of a workplace is the reputation of its employees."

So I spat in her face and walked out. My entire body was shaking from nerves. I was shocked by her spiteful tone, and overtaken by feeling of injustice and exploitation, and that oh-so-familiar sense of dread about the future—a fear that's been with me all my life.

It was pouring with rain that day in the streets around Swéfiéh, but I kept on walking, aimlessly like a zombie, plodding onwards but without any kind of conscious intention. My modest salary had just evaporated, and along with it my dream of finishing university. How on earth could I pay for the fees now? It was out of the question.

I've had so much going on in my head and in my life over the past few months. It hasn't been easy working with that emotionless witch of a boss, always speaking down to us and treating us like slaves. She takes advantage of our weakness and the fact that we rely on her measly wages, and she's always threatening to fire us over the slightest thing, claiming that there are hundreds of girls queuing up to work for her, or even to do the same job for a lower wage. We just have to put up with it, and work overtime whenever she tells us to. We're used to working at weekends and on holidays, and to having our pay docked for whatever trivial reason she thinks up. And we are powerless to complain because we all need the job: there just isn't anything better out there.

I sped up my footsteps, fleeing from a vision of the malicious pleasure my dad takes in hollering at me. The faster I went, the louder his voice rang out in my ears: "*And where's your brothers' share?*" The amount I contribute is never enough; he's always trying to control what's left of my wages. Sometimes it seems like he's jealous of me being able to look after myself, while he himself is struggling to meet our basic needs. He's always putting obstacles in front of me and coming up with problems out of thin air. And he haunted my mind as I ran home—towards him, towards the house, the question going round and round my head, *What am I going to do?*

All I knew was that I couldn't bear to face him. There was no way I could justify losing my job. He would probe for details and would try to find out what happened from my boss. He might just ring her and ask her straight out, or even go round there and ask her to take me back.

I told myself I'd deny whatever she told him and accuse her of lying. Surely he'd believe me? No, I couldn't count on it. Perhaps I'd just tell my mum; she'd give me a bit of breathing space for a few days, and who knows, I might even find another job that could save me from a confrontation with my father.

I should have known that my boss would hear about me and Qais. Girls are such gossips and I haven't been particularly secretive. Especially as I fell in love so bad: I've found it impossible to keep my feelings to myself. I couldn't help sharing snippets about our relationship with my friends at work, letting them know how things were going.

Of course, it's not like I've been going around bragging about it. There were only two girls there that I trusted: one of them was always there to support me, while the other friend warned me to be careful. She was uneasy about the fact that Qais was married, she didn't like the age difference between us, and she didn't believe he would ever leave his wife and ask me to marry him. I didn't listen to her, of course, and I particularly resented the way she put it, in no uncertain terms.

"Hayat, Qais is taking you for a ride. You're still young. Just be really careful."

I'm not young. I'm more mature and aware than most girls my age. Partly because I'm curious by nature and have an intense desire to learn, and partly it's because of the challenges I've had to live through that have made me need to grow up quickly. Life is a harsh teacher, because it makes us sit our exams way before we're ready, before we've even started revising. It forces us to learn from our mistakes and tough experiences, rather than having the luxury of learning from the mistakes of others. Well, let her say what she likes; I'm not your typical nineteen-year-old girl. Life has been hard on me, it's shown no mercy, and I've learnt a lot of lessons the hard way. Never mind the fact that my name means 'life'—life isn't interested in making me any concessions! "Give me a break, life!", I sometimes find myself saying. "Couldn't you be a bit gentler on your namesake?"

Life, Hayat—maybe it's my name that keeps me going. I repeat it to myself in my darkest moments, and it gives me the energy and the will to move forward. But what I'd do for a normal life like other people. I want to live, to soar, and to wipe out the memory of the past. I'm exhausted by the burden on my shoulders, always holding me back. But I won't let it break me, I won't let it!

I broke down into tears once, in the street not far from our house, when a butterfly landed on my shoulder. I saw life in the flutter of its wings and, since that day, I have clung on to life and my right to soar—even if it does sometimes feel like my wings are clipped.

Qais got really frustrated with me the day before yesterday. He's no longer satisfied with just cuddling, touching, and kissing. He wants to penetrate me. He says he wants to feel that our relationship is complete. He doesn't want me to be just half a lover, but a full woman he can form a union with in the same way as he can with his wife. I asked him to wait, to leave his wife first and marry me. I'm not going to squander my virginity before I get married. He didn't like that. He says he can't leave her right now; he still needs a few months to end things with her.

I'm not sure I believe him, although I wish I could have more confidence in him, and part of me wants to give myself to him fully, but I just can't. Maybe it's my friend, the girl from work, or maybe it's the voice of reason, or maybe it's a survival instinct that's stopping me, I don't know, but there is a red line and I know full well that it shouldn't be crossed.

Anyway, my relationship with Qais in no way justifies me losing my job! This is my life and it's my business—that woman has no right to judge me like that. She hasn't got a clue about my relationship with him and neither do I know the ins and outs of his relationship with his wife. I didn't think I could ever allow myself to fall in love with a married man, but I've been drawn into loving him unconsciously, without really reflecting on what the consequences would be.

I needed a man who could restore hope to my life, a knight in shining armour who would deliver me from my father's house and crown me as his queen. But why do I always fall for such losers? I have no idea. Perhaps it's because pleasing my father and putting a smile on his face was a challenge that plagued me throughout my childhood? Or perhaps because my unhappiness finds companionship in other people's misery? I guess it means I don't feel strange in their arms.

Qais was pretty down the day I met him on the Internet. I felt relaxed with him, like I'd never felt with another man before. Our conversation flowed effortlessly, as he talked freely about his life and what was on his mind. He read passages from his life to me like an open book, page after page, without hesitation.

He said he felt suffocated at home with his wife, so he'd turned to the Internet in search of a lifeline. He was looking for someone to open his heart up to, a girl who could bring a smile to his face—something long forgotten. He was right about that: life does sometimes throw a stranger in our path who brings out a smile, when even the people closest to us can't. We both planted that seed of happiness within each other's hearts, but as it grew it turned out to have been the seed of love.

So, the first love of my life is a married man. I've learned to accept this fact and live with it. I understand his circumstances and usually I believe his promises. I have been patient and endured it, hoping that fate would look kindly on me and he would one day make me his wife. I live in the hope of a better life. Real life is too hard without daydreams.

But the day I lost my job, I had no hope; my daydreams were smothered. I was enveloped in a vast, black spider's web, its crippling threads deliberately woven by fate to catch me. One fearsome thread choked off my sense of physical security; another cut off any hope of a better future; a third tightened around me, leaving me vulnerable, easy prey at the mercy of my father.

I walked on and on through the streets of Amman, distracted, aimless. I didn't stop for a bus or a taxi, but kept on going in the pouring rain, plodding on from Swéfiéh to Sports City, as if the growing discomfort in my feet would numb the pain inside, as if the rain would cleanse my wounds and wash away the pain. I willed my feet to hurt more and more to distract me and clear from my mind the fear of the days to come: fear of a life without Qais, fear of an unknown future, fear of my father who waits for my monthly pay packet even more impatiently than I do.

Rana

My mind was also infected with love

HE is like some kind of magnet that pulls my eyes towards him wherever he goes, no matter how I try to resist looking when I know he's nearby. I liked him the first time I clapped eyes on him, and I liked him even more when Hayat told me the feeling was mutual and that he wanted to get to know me. I was as high as a kite until I suddenly realised something else: he's Muslim. His religion is not the same as mine, and we live in a society that allows relationships between the two sexes only within the same religion. Even if I allowed myself to fall in love and get into a relationship with him, it would inevitably be short-lived and would end in heartache. I'm from a conservative Christian family. It's impossible to imagine them condoning a relationship with a Muslim guy.

But Janty won't let me forget him; he is constantly hovering around me at uni. He's always trying to get to know me through friends, sending me love letters from afar. He must be one of the best-looking guys at the university. I particularly like his dark features, his height, and how he dresses. He's got plenty of friends, including girls, and no shortage of admirers.

Well, I guess I've never been one for sticking to the

rules. I'm rebellious by nature, and stubborn; I don't listen to anyone except the voice in my head. I do what I think is right and what makes me happy. Even if that happiness is sometimes a long time in coming. Of course, this isn't easy in a society that restricts a woman's freedom, regardless of her religion, and imposes strict guidelines on how she should live her life, including every aspect of her character and how she should behave in every given situation.

Perhaps it's my personality, or because my mum is foreign, from a different culture, or perhaps it comes from the ethos of the private school I went to, but I'm always very conscious of the contradictory messages I get from the world around me. Everyone seems to want to construct my moral framework for me, in a society that strikes me as schizophrenic and very masculine. Whereas I'm a female, a young woman trying to feed a craving for gender equality and personal freedom. I gather up all the contradictions I see around me and stir them into the melting pot of my personality, mixing them in with what my instinct tells me is right.

I've got used to his bashful glances at me from afar when I'm hanging around with Leila and Hayat in the Business faculty courtyard at our uni, the University of Jordan. Sometimes I forget myself and find myself gazing back, until Hayat's laughter wakes me up from my reverie.

"Who are you staring at?" she laughs. Of course, it's perfectly obvious, and I can't help feeling a bit embarrassed when they catch me drifting off when I'm watching him.

The other day I saw him going into the faculty building

for a lecture, so I tugged them both and hurried them into the lecture hall. It was one of those moments when I kidded myself into thinking there was nothing wrong with me getting to know him as a friend, that a platonic relationship was nothing to be afraid of. I desperately wanted to get to know him up close, and I never wanted those admiring glances to come to an end.

In the end, I took the initiative. I spotted him as soon as I came into the lecture hall. He was sitting in the third row, and the two seats next to him were free. I rushed over to the empty seat next to him and asked him, blushing, if it was reserved for someone else. He smiled and said no. I grabbed Hayat's notebook and put it on the other seat, and asked Leila to quickly go and take the empty seat in the row behind.

"But there are three seats free together there," she started to object. I gave her a look as if to say, "Just do it!"

"Go on," I urged her. "I've already sat down. I'm not moving now."

That was an odd experience, as we sat alongside each other in the lecture hall, strangers, but as if we had known each other for years. My heart raced every time I imagined that he might be just about to strike up a conversation with me. It raced even more when I decided to start it myself. But then I stopped myself at the last minute, as all I could think of to say seemed boring, and the last thing I wanted was to appear dull. He made one comment. I wasn't sure if it was directed at me or not, and I didn't catch exactly what he said, but I nodded and smiled silently, like an idiot.

Outside, after the lecture, I hesitated, and then I headed over to him. He had lit a cigarette and was standing alone near a window. I walked halfway and then almost changed my mind, but it was too late. He saw me approaching and smiled. I babbled like I was speaking for the first time in my life. The words tumbled out of my mouth one at a time, as if they were shy and were waiting to be pushed out. I fumbled about for the right words to utter, anxious to dress them with the right tone of voice, not too warm or too cold.

"Hi. Could I possibly borrow your notes to photocopy them? I didn't catch everything he said."

He replied with a beaming smile. I sensed his embarrassment, too, as though he couldn't quite believe what was happening. The girl he had had his eye on for months had just walked up and asked to borrow his notes? It clearly meant just one thing: that the feeling was mutual.

"Of course you can. If you want, we could go and copy them together?"

Like a kid playing with fire, I felt a tingle of excitement mixed with fear. I moved closer to him, gingerly, cautiously watching my steps and my words. The closer I got, the more I felt his warmth, and the more I felt that warmth, the more I craved heat, like a piece of ice longing to evaporate.

We didn't exactly make the most of those few minutes to get to know each other on our way to the photocopying room. We were both just a bundle of nerves. But we realised that even though we stumbled over our words, our hearts were somehow deep in conversation, in their own secret language that was plain to see on our faces and in our gestures. We realised that we both felt strangely comfortable side by side: a feeling I don't think either of us had ever really felt before.

To my surprise, when we went our separate ways afterwards, my head was pounding, as if I was addicted to his presence after just one dose. I felt intoxicated, staggering between a heart that was drawn to a man who was forbidden, a body that longed to inhale the heavenly breath of love, and a rational mind trying to corral those two instincts into behaving sensibly.

Or so I thought at the beginning, until I realised it was too late and I was already infected with love. Any logical capacities I had ever possessed were warped by this fever as I fell under his seductive power.

PART TWO

LEILA

BARELY a few days had passed since I got my exam results before my mum started piling on the pressure about finding a job. It wasn't my future career or the salary she was thinking about, although my parents would certainly be glad of the extra income. No, her main concern was about me securing the best chances of bagging a husband.

Most men looking to get married these days are unable to support a family on their income alone, so they hope to find a wife who can help share the financial burden of raising children. This has ironic implications for women in our society: our hard-won right to go out to work has turned into a duty, another chore that doesn't reduce the long list of other chores waiting for us at home. A working woman is still a housewife, too. It has become expected of women now that they should do the housework, tend to the needs of their husband and children, and somehow find the energy for a job outside the home. They have to juggle all these demands at the same time. Meanwhile, men only have to focus on their jobs and on providing for the family financially. A Jordanian man isn't ashamed of accepting his wife's help economically, but it would be shameful for him to help share her burden of cleaning, cooking, and washing.

A man is considered a good catch if he has a job with a good salary. Meanwhile, to qualify as a potential bride, a woman has to be beautiful, the right age, morally impeccable, a talented cook and cleaner, and have a degree and a job. Maximising the chances of finding a fiancé is a very difficult and complex game, so a job has become a precondition.

My sister Salma was extremely frustrated, though, by the response when she got a promotion last month. She had expected everyone to be delighted and to want to celebrate her success with her, but she was shocked by people's reaction, just as I was when I finished my degree—with a distinction, no less! She had also failed to see the bigger picture, namely that the ultimate goal is to find a husband, not to progress in your career. Instead of being showered with blessings, she faced a hailstorm of reproach and warnings. Most people think that the higher a woman gets promoted, the less chance she has of ever getting married!

What kind of madness is this? The logic is that a Jordanian man would never marry a woman with a higher salary or a more important job than his. It must be an inferiority complex. In our society's public consciousness, the man is still seen as superior, and a woman is only worthy of praise and admiration when her good fortune and success are shared with her husband. The man is the master of the house and it is he who holds the reins of power, including the purse strings, even if the financial role has become more difficult for men these days.

As for me, I assumed my first-class degree would make it much easier to find a job. I was pretty confident that I would find something suitable without too much trouble, although everyone around me seemed intent on crushing my optimism with talk of the economic crisis and the need for contacts.

"No one can get a job these days!"

"If you don't have contacts, there's no way you'll find a job!"

But I refused to listen to them. I found advice online about how to write a CV, and I included a bullet point you couldn't miss about coming top in my year. I started sending it off here and there, and it was only two days before companies started contacting me to ask me in for an interview.

I was delighted when I got offered a position in a bank. It's seen as a respectable job for a girl and a sensible working environment, with reasonable hours, meaning it meets society's requirements for a woman to work and be a housewife at the same time. And, of course, my mum was over the moon and immediately started showing off to all her friends.

I didn't know what to expect of my first day at work, because I'd never had a job before. It was a mix of excitement, terror, and feeling alone. I felt like an outsider in a system made up of hundreds of people who all seemed to know precisely how to behave in an exact and measured way, according to an agreed plan they were all party to and knew like the back of their hands. I was the youngest by far. I watched everyone, I watched my footsteps, and I tried to make sense of the baffling instructions I was given.

***

My boss is middle-aged, quite short, with white hair. They call him Abu Issam ('Issam's dad'), but I'm wary of being so familiar with him. I would usually address a man his age as *amu*, 'uncle,' but now, in a different context, a work environment, *amu* might be inappropriate. But I'm also embarrassed to call him Abu Issam.

Abu Issam, on the other hand, has no concept of shame. Nothing gives him any cause to feel ashamed, regardless of his position, his age, the age difference between us, or even the fact that his son Issam is the same age as me. He is constantly looking at me in a creepy way that makes me feel really uncomfortable. I wouldn't want to misinterpret his looks or rush to judge him, but the way he stares at me makes me feel flustered and desperate to escape from his office. And that just makes him grin and stare at me all the more. Perhaps my discomfort turns him on, or perhaps he interprets my reaction somehow as a green light to pursue his prey.

He is always giving off contradictory signals. Sometimes he treats me like a daughter, taking on a fatherly role, and sometimes he exploits the fact that I've let down my defences to reach out and touch me. He tries to make it look accidental, and his age helps him pass it off as a paternal gesture, but I shudder when I feel him press against me; I'm amazed at his brazenness. He knows that his authority makes him infallible and gives him free rein to harass me.

I've been agonising over what to do. This is my first job and it's the first time I've found myself trapped in such a horrible, humiliating situation. I've tried to ignore it and push it out of my mind, but he just won't leave me alone. I know I can't escalate things within the bank, because my reputation is at stake. After all, he is a man and, no matter what happens, as a man he won't be judged as harshly as I am; even though I am the victim, I'm the one being violated. I've been wondering about telling my dad. Or maybe my brother? But do I really dare speak out and risk exposing my family and friends to trouble they could certainly do without?

I've started to count the hours until I can leave at the end of the day. I'm getting used to the palpitations every morning. I'm always on tenterhooks, listening out for Abu Issam's footsteps, trembling like a kitten trapped in a corner, anxiously looking for a way to escape. I've started to change the way I dress, doing everything I can to downplay my appearance. I've stopped wearing my knee-length skirt and now only wear a much longer one.

I've even been considering the veil as a last ditch attempt to protect myself, because some men do judge women by their appearance and Abu Issam might be reading something into what I wear, thinking I'm encouraging him. In fact, I've been wondering about the veil for some time now. I try to adhere to the teachings of my religion and to fulfil the duties expected of me, and I do believe that the veil is one of them. I find comfort in prayer, which has been part of my life since I was a child, but I am somehow slightly terrified of the veil. Although I believe in the importance of it as a tenet of our faith, it's not as simple as that. It's a big decision that you can't just go back on; it's a decision you make for life, like marriage. If I choose to wear one, it will affect every aspect of my life, changing forever the way people see me and how I see myself.

The other day when I got home, after closing the door to my room behind me, I found a stretch of fabric and started to wrap it around my head. I stared at myself in the mirror.

"Am I still pretty like this?" I asked my reflection. My nose was first to reply. It stood out more than usual, as though it had assumed a bigger area of my face. Horrified, I pulled off the fabric and flung it aside, spreading my hair out over my shoulders. Picking up my brush, I gently combed it, carefully smoothing it out. My hair, with its rich colour and delicate curls, is what makes me who I am, what makes me feminine. Like any other woman, of course I care about my looks and want to be beautiful. I love it if I get an admiring glance; it's a little buzz which reminds me of my femininity.

I could never be described as strikingly beautiful, but I've learned over the years how to take care of my appearance and make the best of my features, and how to emphasise my femininity. I think my hair is my best weapon, and having my hair done always makes me feel great, like a new woman. At the end of the day, every woman wants to look attractive, and her hair is one of her most important assets. I do worry that wearing a veil would hide away my best feature and make me less pretty. And I'm afraid that it could also reduce my chances of finding a husband.

I had previously decided to put off the issue of the veil until after I'd got married, but now I've started thinking about it again. Perhaps this whole Abu Issam thing is a test from God, or punishment from him, or a sign to remind me that the veil is important and that I shouldn't put it off. This is a tough decision, one of the most difficult I've ever taken, with perhaps the most impact.

So in the end I approached my mother about the veil. I needed her help to decide what to do. But I was surprised by her frosty reaction. I had expected her to be pleased I was considering it, at least. In fact, I genuinely imagined she'd throw her arms around me and congratulate me, or even shriek with joy, and then rush to brag to her friends about how mature I was being, taking my religion so seriously.

But once again, I completely misjudged how she'd take it, and how she sees the issue. I realised she is really worried about me. She shares the responsibility for me finding a husband, after all. If I fail, she fails too, and my fears are her fears. Or perhaps it's the other way round? Her fears fill me with fear, and if she fails in her role it means I'll be a failure, too.

She already blames herself for failing Salma, as far as she's concerned, and she's determined to make up for it with me. She worries that if I wear a veil I'll have much less chance of getting married. So she asked me to put it off for a while. I was just about to tell her about Abu Issam, but she beat me to it and started telling me instead about a possible suitor.

Oum Mohammed, our neighbor, has a young male relative who's looking for a bride. Oum Mohammed approached my mother about him and filled her in on the essentials, namely his social status and financial situation. He's from a good family, apparently: they have a food-manufacturing business that this guy runs together with his father and two brothers. He's the oldest brother. He studied in England and now he's looking for a nice girl to settle down with and have a family.

Of course, I'm the 'nice' girl in question here. I'm the one who now has to steel herself for a gruelling inspection visit from this guy and his family so they can judge whether I'm 'nice' enough. We'll all have to dress up and look our best, my entire family and I, to try and impress the groom and his family. My mum will sing my praises and list all my assets, and his mother will do the same for him. My mum will harp on about my looks, my manners, my extraordinary housework skills, while his mum will dwell on their family's wealth, the guy's degree, his job, and his future prospects.

I've seen it all before. I'll have to bring round coffee and sit demurely while the two families bat the conversation back and forth. I'll follow the ball being passed between the two sides, mostly in silence, sometimes uttering a murmur, trying to sound interested. In fact, I am the ball being knocked back and forth, which they are at liberty to dissect and scrutinise. Each side takes it in turns to serve while the other receives the shot. I nod my head from time to time and keep a permanent smile on my face, which I exaggerate whenever anyone catches my eye.

I don't usually object to anything my mum says on these occasions, although it often seems like she's talking about someone else with the same name as me and who, bizarrely, has quite a lot in common with me, yet otherwise has nothing to do with me. The fascinating anecdotes she narrates so eloquently form wonderful stories which I'd love to hear, if it weren't for the fact that I'm supposedly the heroine.

To be honest, I'm sick of this same old scene repeating *ad nauseam*. This won't be the first time I've dolled myself up to go on display like this. We're used to suitors knocking on our door from time to time, though nothing ever seems to come of it. And a few years ago, I saw them come and go, all asking for Salma's hand in marriage, and I'd watch her reject them all, as she tried to shun the whole situation. She couldn't stand this traditional approach to arranging marriages. She felt humiliated by the charade of putting herself on public display for them to decide if she was good enough. And now it's my turn to be in the same position, over and over again. Every time a suitor is proposed I try to object, but my mum never lets me have any say in the matter. She gives the family an appointment, and then it's a *fait accompli*, and I can't get out of it.

The tension in the house lasts for days after the family visit. After the suitor has left, my mum then implements her strategy of persuasion and intimidation to try and convince me to accept his offer, regardless of what I think of him. She insists I shouldn't rule him out at first sight, that I should give him a chance and get to know him a bit more. She lists all his plus points, as highlighted by his mother, and emphasises his strong financial position and the comfortable life I'll have with him.

But this time I put my foot down: I knew he was not the one for me and I told her I would not accept. My mum's face changed. Her brow filled with black lines, ominously warning me of the dark times ahead. The black lines of her scowl foretold the exhaustion and misery I would face as the candle of my career aspirations burned out, leaving me alone in the shadows with no husband to bring light to my life. Black lines that warned of loneliness and longing for love and a family. The dark furrows grew more intense as I continued to dig my heels in. As though squeezing the last black ink from a pen cartridge, she eked out enough to play one last card, which she thrust in my face. Huge letters spelled out the word *aanis*: 'spinster.'

Of course, I understand her concern for me and Salma. I understand the pressure on us to accept this opportunity that has knocked on our door. And yet I cannot force myself to accept someone whom my heart rejects. I can't just 'give him a chance,' like my mum always says, no matter how much they go on about his wealth and everything he's got going for him. How can I agree to live with someone I don't love? How can I devote my life to a man who doesn't mean anything to me?

I am not in the slightest bit convinced when they say that love comes after marriage. Other girls might be content to wait and see, but not me. I have been trying to listen to what my mum's saying, but the psychological pressure is wearing me down, robbing me of the strength to think and decide.

***

Today's been a tough day at work. Abu Issam started treating me differently, giving me the cold shoulder and seizing on any chance to find mistakes in my calculations and punish me. I admit I was quite distracted, thinking about what my mother said, and about the 'golden apple of an opportunity waiting to be picked,' as she put it, and as a result I made a few serious errors.

I succumbed to the pressure at one point and burst into tears. I quickly pulled myself together when Ali walked into the office. I wiped away my tears and forced a smile, trying to make my voice sound cheerful as I said hello. But I couldn't really hide it from him; he could see from my expression and my red eyes that something was wrong. The truth is I didn't intend to hide it from him completely, probably because subconsciously I was craving his sympathy and looking for a way to get closer to him.

Ali is an Iraqi customer who comes into the bank from time to time to carry out transactions and check his accounts. A kind of friendship has developed between us during his frequent visits over the past few months. He tells me what's on his mind and about how he misses life in Baghdad. And I tell him what's on my mind, about my life in Amman and my dreams for the future.

He wanted to know why I was upset. I tried to avoid answering, but he insisted, saying he couldn't stand to see me sad like this, and that it made him feel terrible to see me cry. I was touched that he seemed genuinely concerned about me, so I opened up and told him about the Abu Issam problem in as objective a way as I could.

As I talked to him, I tried to distance a certain image from my mind: that image of me as a dreamy princess and him as a knight astride his stallion. My days have been full of daydreams like this in the last few months. I imagine him as a friend, a husband, a lover. I keep finding myself composing fanciful stories, spin-offs of the romance novels I devoured as a teenager, as whimsical as building castles in the air. I've been dreaming of scenarios where things between us could take a new direction, where he tells me how much he likes me. If only we could swap roles, and I could be the man and be open in declaring how I feel about him.

If I were the man, I would let myself be led by my heart. I'd unleash my tongue to express my feelings. But I'm not. I am a woman. I have to beat around the bush, offer subtle signals for him to pick up, patiently hoping he'll notice and understand. All a woman can do is coyly leave her door ever so slightly ajar, so that she isn't thought of as cheap and worthless. Because as a woman, I am only worth what I can fetch when sold to whoever wants me, and my value plummets if I openly offer myself or reveal my desire.

But today there was no time for any more subtle signals, or waiting patiently and praying. Today I put him on the spot. His reaction could have extinguished every one of my hopes and dreams, finally making me trudge back home to my mother to tell her that I agreed to accept her suitor. I let my tears fall.

I could no longer distinguish fact from fiction, reality

from my daydreams, when I heard him utter the question that was my lifeline:

"Leila, will you marry me?"

ALI

A way of life I'm forced to follow

I left Leila feeling stunned by the sudden developments. I didn't think I'd ever hear myself asking that question. I had gone over it in my head hundreds of times before, but whenever I convinced myself to do it, I would hesitate and put it off, telling myself things might change, or a miracle might happen and the need to get married might suddenly disappear.

I threw out the question like someone throwing himself into the sea and as though blasted by the cold of the water, I froze—numb, emotionless—and barely noticed her surprise or the hysterical reaction that followed. I did what I needed to do and now it was up to fate to guide me as it saw fit.

The traffic light ahead turns red, and the cars line up one behind the other—all the various makes and colours. An inquisitive child catches my eye, staring at me from the back seat of the car next to mine. He is sitting behind his father and his mother is on the back seat beside him. The three of them fit perfectly with the idyllic image of a happy family that I've long had embedded in my mind.

The image scrambles up in my mind then reforms with me as the child. I see my father, back from the grave, and my mum has lost all traces of age. What a beautiful scene:

the epitome of humanity captured in those three people. The image then forms again in my mind, and this time I am the father, Leila is at my side, and our child sits in the back.

I keep reminding myself of the admiring way she always looks at me, the personal interest she clearly shows towards me, and how she puts me at ease with her friendly way of talking. I enjoy talking to her and feel like we're close. Our friendship means a lot to me, and I've always told myself so. If I am going to get married someday, then I would want Leila to be my bride. She is one of the sweetest people I have ever met, and if I wanted a mother for my children I can't imagine finding anyone better. But I can't help wondering if I can really provide a happy life for this beautiful woman? Will I really have saved her from the miserable life she sees ahead of her or have I dragged her into one that may be even worse?

I know that despite my decision, I won't be able to sacrifice my heart, and I know I will be deceiving her in one of the most fundamental aspects of married life. But I am also sure that I will do everything in my power to make her happy and to provide her with a decent life. I will certainly strive to be a good husband and a good father.

My mum will be over the moon, of course. She'll finally see her eldest son married and have her dreams come true of a grandson to inherit the family name. I know she'd prefer my bride to be Iraqi, but she won't mind me marrying someone of another nationality, especially now after all these years of me putting it off and shunning the idea. I really want to make her happy, and perhaps it will help her get fit again after her health has suffered so much since we left Iraq.

We've been through a lot in the past few years. Iraq got even worse after the end of the war and the fall of Saddam Hussein's regime. Armed gangs took control of the country, and our property and our jobs were no longer safe. Life became significantly more dangerous and the threatening letters became more frequent.

My mother had a breakdown the day my uncle was kidnapped. Days went by when she hovered between reality and her fantasy world, unable to differentiate between the two. She was lost in her memories, carried back to 1984 when we lost my father in the Iran-Iraq war. She would have lost grip of reality altogether were it not for her natural instinct as a mother kicking in. She needed her full mental and physical strength to look after three children on her own. I'm the oldest: I was ten then, and my twin sisters were five.

It would be the end of her if anything ever happened to my uncle again. When he was kidnapped, she suffered from hallucinations and visions until he was returned to us two weeks later. The family rallied round and managed to raise the huge sum required for the ransom. We didn't truly believe we would ever see him again, until the day he stood there at our door, safe and sound, shouting for joy, because there had been so many cases of people paying the ransom and still never seeing their family again.

But after that, things became unbearable. We all lived in constant fear for our lives. We couldn't afford $100,000 again if anyone else was kidnapped. Next time, we knew we would never see them again. We started making plans to leave the country, but it happened in a way we never imagined.

We received a message threatening to kidnap me, and that was the last straw for my mum. She couldn't wait a moment longer. She started screaming hysterically and insisted on leaving the house that day without stopping to think. We didn't have time to say goodbye to any of our friends or family. We grabbed the essentials, and had to leave behind a lot of stuff that was precious to us. We got a taxi, bid farewell to life as we knew it, and set off for Jordan.

The early days were tough after we arrived in Amman. It wasn't easy to adapt to our new way of life. My mum's health really went downhill, and we no longer had access to our money in Iraq. Most of our income was from real estate in Baghdad, but we couldn't collect the rent at the time. Things were really tight and we could no longer afford my mother's medication. We went to the charities that help Iraqi refugees, and after a long and difficult period, my mother's health eventually began to improve, and so did our finances and life more generally.

Throughout that period, my mother kept on nagging me to get married. It became something she was obsessed with, that filled all her thoughts and took up the lion's share of our conversation. She kept saying that seeing me get married was her greatest dream, and that her chief concern before she departed this world was to get me and my sisters set up, and to see us all happy in our own homes, with our own families.

So, now I'm making her dream come true. I'm making Leila's dream of getting married come true, too. And I'm making my dream of having a family come true. I'm following the path of social convention, after all—doing what is expected of a man my age. It's a way of life I'm forced to follow, regardless of my real sexual inclination and my personal needs.

***

My mum put her hand to her mouth and let out a loud, trilling shriek. Tears of joy filled her eyes and she started pouring out questions about the girl who had 'rung the doorbell of my heart,' as she put it. She wanted to know everything about her—her figure; her social standing; her education; her height; the colour of her skin, hair, and eyes. It was as if it was her getting married, not me, as if the clock had turned back and she was once again putting on her white dress to walk down the aisle. As they say, the groom's mother is also the bride.

I couldn't share her joy, though. Quite the opposite. All I felt and all I feel now is fear taking hold of me and pressing on my nerves. I'm setting off on a path that will be a major test of how well I can lie. It's a lie I'm used to living with, but living it with someone else means taking it to another level. I wear my lie like a professional: it masks every bit of me and I take on the persona of a man who is not me, a man whose true face very few people know. I'm about to progress to a much more difficult stage where there's a much greater risk of revealing that hidden face if I waver and play my role like anything less than a professional.

We all get used to wearing masks in our lives so that we can blend in with the crowd. It's a heavy burden to bear full-time, and when you have to wear that mask even in the presence of the people closest to you, it becomes even heavier, more fragile, and more difficult to carry. You need to be more alert than ever, careful not to drop your guard in a moment of forgetfulness.

So here I am, taking my mask with me from my mother's house to my future marital home, embarking on a life that may well be impossible to live without it.

HAYAT

I should have known that the torment I endured for years was not over yet

YOU'RE more vulnerable to sickness when your life turns sour and you lose all hope. It makes you reset your clock somehow, as you realise that as long as your heart is still beating and your feet can still walk, then your heartbeat will always be there to guide you, like a beam of light from a lighthouse leading you to safety.

I was weak with exhaustion after hours of walking in the cold and the rain. My body refused to give up until I reached my bed, where I collapsed, lifeless like a corpse, shivering furiously in an attempt to expel the cold from my bones. As my temperature rose, the heat made my thoughts sizzle like they were cooking in a pot over the fire, evaporating into bubbles of hallucinations. I felt like it would burn me up altogether, were it not for the cold water compress my mother pressed against my forehead through the night until the morning light appeared at dawn.

Every cloud has a silver lining, I told myself. The fever had saved me from having to think of a convincing pretext to explain to my father why I hadn't gone to work that day. But it wasn't enough to excuse me from the dinner party my family was invited to at his friend's farm that evening.

Dad likes us to give the outward impression that we're your average happy family. He insists on rounding us all up for every special occasion or when we see friends or family. I remember once, three years ago, when I refused to go with him to visit my grandmother, and the only response I got was a slap so hard that I can still hear the blow ringing in my ears.

The heat gradually dissipated from my body, dispersing like clouds, while the volatile Amman weather changed from downpours to bright sunshine in a matter of hours. I started to feel better as dusk fell. I got up out of bed and stood under a hot shower, before I started to get ready for the evening. I put on blue jeans and a black blouse that goes well with my olive skin tone. I found my delicate butterfly earrings, and as I put them on, I looked in the mirror to check that my father would be happy with my appearance. I'm used to him constantly objecting whenever I'm just about to leave the house.

Abu George's farm is near Madaba, about an hour's drive south of Amman. It's a beautiful spot and he invites us over fairly regularly. The two families gathered around the fire for a barbecue. My mother and I sat with George's mum, Oum George, and we cut the meat up and put it on skewers, placing a piece of tomato and onion between each chunk of meat. Then we passed the kebabs to one of the men to grill over the hot coal. My two younger brothers were busy playing with a ball, while my dad, Abu George, and his son George sat around a table playing backgammon. I set myself up with the shisha pipe and sat back to take in the scenery. I tried to clear my mind and just enjoy the moment.

Dad started drinking beer the minute we arrived at the farm. We're used to seeing him drunk, especially on occasions like this. My mother kept an eye on him, trying to persuade him not to drink too much, but he paid no attention to her. Oum George offered me a glass of beer with the food. My mum tried to object, but my father interrupted.

"Let the girl relax!"

I seized the glass from her hand and gulped it down like an alcoholic, ignoring the bitter taste as it poured down my throat. I was in dire need of something strong, although I had never actually tried alcohol before and immediately felt its effect. I wanted to lose my mind that night like my father did, and I ignored my mother's anxious glances.

My little brothers got tired of playing. Sleepily, they curled up on my mum's lap; she was also tired. My father was tipsy and wasn't interested in going home yet. George wanted to head back to Amman to spend the rest of the evening with his friends. My mother asked him to drop them off on his way and he didn't mind. She wanted me to come back with them, but I didn't feel like leaving yet.

I wanted to stay away from home for as long as possible. I wanted those few hours to stretch out forever, so I would never need to go back and confront my problems that lurked there. I wanted her to wait a while and for us all to go back together, because I was wary of going back on my own with my dad, but the effect of the beer seemed to stop me from making a sensible decision.

We left two hours later. It was one o'clock in the morning. I stood by the farm gate, waiting for my father as he said goodbye to Abu George and Oum George, thanking them for a lovely evening. He walked towards me, staring at me with a look that suddenly took me back. That look that I thought I had buried along with all those painful memories. I thought it had disappeared from my life years ago, never to return, although it persists in the terrifying nightmares which haunt me with disturbing frequency.

"So, who's a big girl now, then?" he said as he came closer, and whispered in my ear. "You've started drinking, too?"

I felt queasy when I smelt the alcohol on his breath. Paralysed with fear, I didn't know how to respond. My heart began to race, as desperate as me to escape, as though it had a clearer memory than I did of what he used to do in those days.

"You want me to give you a driving lesson?" he asked.

I shook my head, racking my brains for a way out of this awful situation. For a few minutes, I managed to convince myself that I'd probably misread the way he was looking at me, or that it was a fleeting look that had passed, that he really had changed dramatically in the past few months.

But unfortunately, my instinct was not mistaken. I should have known that the torment I endured for years was not over yet. I should have known that this would obliterate any feeling of safety, leaving me lost, crushed beneath the world's feet, ripped to shreds by its teeth. Later it would seem that fate had conspired to play along with him that night, and the moon didn't stand by passively, either. They all ganged up together to play some satanic game in which I was the victim.

The Madaba – Dead Sea road was pitch black, with no street lamps to light the way. The moon chose to hide that night and was nowhere to be seen. Perhaps the moon had given my father her blessing for his crime, or perhaps she was ashamed to witness it. I was alone with my father. I drove in silence, praying to God over and over in my heart, begging him to stand at my side and let me get through the night safely. But God did not listen. He also hid and abandoned me to my destiny.

I was completely alone when my father started to run his hand across my thigh.

"Dad, what are you doing?" I asked him, my voice tinged with horror. There was no doubt now of the peril I was in. He told me off sternly and ordered me to carry on driving as though nothing had happened, as though it were someone else's body his hand had violated, not mine. He leant back in his seat beside me and reached over to touch my breasts with his fingers.

He was so immersed in savoring the body of a mistress he had missed these past few years, that he was oblivious to the desperation on her face: the desperate expression of a woman for whom the world had turned to black, and who could find refuge only in death.

For years and years, I promised myself daily that I would never allow him to touch me again. And here he was exerting his control over me like he always did. But that night, behind the steering wheel, I realised that even though the best way to undermine his intentions would be to convince myself to carry on living like a normal human being, in fact I knew I would prefer death to this.

I spotted a large truck hurtling towards us at great speed. I made my decision as fast as lightning. As my lips uttered the words of the Shahada prayer, my foot pressed the accelerator and my hands turned the steering wheel towards the truck.

Given the amount of alcohol coursing through his veins, my father was incredibly quick to realise what I was doing. He flung himself at me with all his strength, wresting the steering wheel from my hands. He slammed his foot down over mine onto the brake in a split-second movement like a thread splitting life from death. He was silent for a moment, then exploded into a fury like I'd never seen before, and I had seen a lot from him. He reached out, slapped me, then hit me again and again, before he dragged me out of the car and threw me onto the ground, shouting and swearing and cursing.

It was several minutes before he calmed down. I got back into the car, the passenger seat this time, in the belief that what had happened would have killed any desire he felt that night. I expected him to turn around and take us back home, but, to my horror, he carried on driving along the same dark road until he found a smaller dirt track leading off it. He turned off, mumbling incomprehensibly under his breath.

I jumped to my feet the moment he stopped the car. I decided to run—it was my only hope. He chased after me, screaming a barrage of threats and insults. Suddenly, he stopped, caught his breath, and threatened me at the top of his voice: if I ran away, he would call the police and tell them I had run off with a man, and he would kill me to spare his honour.

I didn't know what to do. I knew very well that this wasn't beyond him. I stopped, I had to catch my breath too, and there was just a short distance between me and him. Sensing I was starting to give in, he played the last card in his hand, and brought my mum into it.

"You can run as much as you like. Your mother's at home. I'll just go and do to her what I wanted to do to you. And more."

"Dad, why are you doing this?" I said, trying to appeal to his mercy. "I'm Hayat… your daughter." I looked into his eyes, hoping to stir just a glimmer of humanity in his heart.

He lunged at me and tried to pull me towards to him, while I pulled away with all my might.

"Don't you remember when I was born?" I pleaded. "You… you… you called me Hayat… Hayat… I'm Hayat, your little girl."

But he didn't listen and he didn't remember. The only thing on his mind was to find a way to beat me down and make me submit. He came closer and closer, until he had me in his grip and could throw me down to the ground again. He launched himself on me with his full force, tearing at my clothes, stripping me naked, while I did everything I could to resist, screaming and struggling to get away. He muffled my screams with his hand and restrained me with the weight of his body. The only response my body had left was my tears that fell to the ground, the silent witness to the horror.

And then he stopped. As if the nightmare had been interrupted, as if nothing had happened. He called me back to the car and drove me home. In silence.

PART THREE

SALMA

All I see in their eyes is pity

THE news of Leila's engagement hits me like a slap in the face.

She comes home one day bouncing with happiness, skipping aimlessly from one room to another. She hugs me tight and smothers me with kisses, gushing about how much she loves me.

"You're the best sister in the whole world!"

I'm amazed by this flood of emotion. We're close and we love each other, but we don't often show it as effusively as this. I look her in the eyes, wondering where this emotion has come from; I've never seen her as excited as this before.

"Guess what happened!"

"I don't know! What? Tell me!"

"Remember the lovely Iraqi guy I told you about? Well… he asked me to marry him!"

I can't believe my ears. It was only this morning I was thinking that Leila's no longer a little girl and her time will come soon. But this? This is like a stab in the back. This is a painful blow I am going to have to stomach in silence. I know I should be happy for my sister—this is the most important event in her life, this news holds the key to her future, and mine. But instead of picturing Leila as the beautiful bride, the only image I can see is of me, all alone. There are so many reasons I ought to share her joy—tradition, logic, and solidarity with my sister—but in fact all I feel is fear and jealousy.

"You're kidding!"

I try to sound excited, as though I can't believe such amazing news. I give her a huge hug and burst into tears. I can't hide this maelstrom of emotions inside me, but I feel terrible to be crying so I try to make it seem like they're tears of joy for my little sister.

***

Her engagement seems interminable. It's hard work continually faking enthusiasm so that no one notices how jealous I am, but I do it without even realising. I'm her older sister and the closest person to her, so I know I should be open and honest with her. But instead I'm extremely cautious about expressing an opinion, and I'm careful to stay upbeat and supportive whenever she's worried or apprehensive about her future life.

What bothers me the most is the looks I get all the time now that both my brother and my little sister have found spouses before me. I also find it very irritating the way people criticise my mother for marrying off my younger sister before me. She always finds a diplomatic response: "It's fate. We can't stand in the way of fate."

But all I can see in their eyes is pity. I sense them searching for the right words when they're talking to me. Perhaps I'm being overly sensitive, and reflecting what I feel inside onto the people around me, but I can no longer look anyone in the eye. I feel like such a failure.

I'm dreading the day of the wedding, when the guests are going to gaze at me with that pitying look which translates as the one phrase I absolutely cannot stand: "*O'balek*. I wish the same for you." I feel like pasting a set response on my forehead for every time someone reassures me it's my turn next: "Yeah, fuck you."

RANA

I couldn't exactly leave him in that state

THE weeks flew by, and things between me and Janty developed astonishingly quickly, though we skirted around discussing the precise nature of our relationship. We were enjoying just talking and getting to know each other without setting things in stone. We started to spend more and more time together within the safe confines of the university, and I found I liked him more with every hour we spent together.

News of our relationship started to spread among the students. Everyone was itching to know what was going on and couldn't help joining in the gossip. The rumours reached my cousin in the medical faculty who saw it as an opportunity to express his masculinity and flex his muscles at us. Overnight the dynamics between me and my cousin transformed from brotherly friendship into the relationship between suspect and prosecutor, a relationship dominated by secrecy and lies.

My cousin summoned Janty and me to meet him for coffee. He had stepped into the shoes of my concerned older relative, the man of the family, guardian of our family honour. Frankly, the shoes were too big for him; the look didn't suit him at his age. I'd never seen this side of him before. We're almost exactly the same age, and the question of honour is about as far as you can get from what normally comes up in our conversation. But today he was acting like someone else, someone I didn't know, someone who had assumed responsibility for defining my social boundaries and who felt he had the right and the power to make emotional decisions on my behalf.

He claimed it was his prerogative to intervene in this serious personal matter in my life. He said all this as if completely oblivious to the other person sitting right next to me, the man who had captured my heart, who had won me over with his chivalrous persistence. But now I saw Janty trapped in an awkward corner, unable to object or protest when my cousin spoke of tribal sentiments and honour. He must have thought that if he wanted to join the world of grown-ups, he had to play their game. It is just a game, a kind of machismo contest where they all vie to dominate the females of the herd. To them, my love for Janty is nothing more than one man threatening the property of another. An insult to the men of my family. They all swarm together like pins around a magnet, never mind the quarrel over inheritance that normally comes between them.

I'm a woman, and as a female I carry the family's honour; I am obliged to protect it. But this honour is a fortress that no outsider is trusted to enter. Every male member of the family sees himself as a sentry guard, watching us like hawks, ready to pull us up any time we cross their red lines that dictate how we can and can't behave.

Honour is something fragile, prone to being shattered.

And yet, bizarrely, it is also flexible, and the men knead it like dough into whatever shape suits them and helps them exert their control over the women, whether it's imposing a special dress code; dictating where, and when, and how they can leave the house; or exercising a veto over their choice of friends, male or female.

Today, Janty and I were obliged to obey his orders, even if only for appearance's sake. Janty apologised to my cousin and promised to keep his distance. But our feelings refused to apologise; inside, neither of us was ready to comply. We knew there was nothing we could do: we couldn't stand up to him and refuse to let him hurt us. The only solution was to be more careful around the university and be stricter about how and when we met, to keep things out of the public eye.

We were playing with fire, and the fire was playing with us. Trying to be restrained just kindled the flames inside us. We spent our time together at uni in the company of a chaperone to demonstrate that it was just a platonic relationship, not a love affair. Hayat and Leila became the third party in our relationship, which couldn't exist without one of them being present; if one of them left, we had to go our separate ways, too.

We started to dream of some free time that we could spend together, but alone, and we started to make plans in such meticulous detail it was as if we were planning a wedding. His family owns another apartment in the Rashid suburb near the university campus. It isn't rented out at the moment, so Janty suggested that we met there. I refused at first, afraid that someone might see us together and tell a member of my family. I was also afraid of being alone with him. I knew how strong my feelings were and how weak I was in the face of this attraction; I couldn't trust myself or him to be able to resist the desire we both felt.

Then came that fateful day. We were standing in the courtyard of the Business faculty—Janty and I, and Leila and Hayat. It was the break between lectures, so the courtyard was full of students moving between classrooms. I was deep in conversation with Janty when all of a sudden I felt some shameless bastard touch my backside: it was a student, walking past with two of his friends. He just reached out and pressed his hand against my ass, as quick as a flash, and then walked on as if nothing had happened. The shock must have shown on my face, though I didn't mean to let it, and Janty noticed.

"What's wrong?" he asked. "What happened?"

I sensed that I should stifle my anger, so I kept quiet about this fleeting assault. I suspected that if I told Janty, he'd see it as a test of his manhood. He'd feel compelled to start a fight with him, and he might come out of it the worse off.

"Nothing. I'm fine," I said, knowing full well that he wouldn't believe me. My body language had already given it away. Without waiting for an answer from me, he flew off the handle and in a split second he was off after him.

I was terrified as I saw Janty chase after the student and push him forcefully to the ground. I was rooted to the spot, watching a volley of punches fly between him and Janty. The surprise gave Janty the advantage at first, and he managed to deal him some strong blows to the face, but the student's two friends quickly entered the fray, knocking Janty to the ground, leaving him unable to protect himself from the torrent of kicks from the three of them.

A large crowd of students started to gather around the fight. Then, after a lot of effort, a group of guys managed to pull them apart and get Janty out. A few seconds later, Janty's friends appeared and gathered around him. The Circassian students at the university are used to having to defend themselves, and they always stand up for each other. It's the same among large families and among students who come to Amman from the same home town. It's an opportunity for them all to flex their muscles and demonstrate their loyalty to the clan.

Suddenly, two huge menacing groups had amassed and were head to head. I realised then that I might have inadvertently sparked a bloodbath that could have untold casualties. And the biggest victim would be my reputation.

My heart froze when I saw Janty's face: it was swollen, cut, and bruised, and he was the same all over his body. But I kept my cool, knowing I would have to act quickly before things got out of hand. Confidently, I walked over to Janty.

"If you don't sort this out and stop this nonsense right now, then you'll never hear my voice again," I threatened. "I'm not prepared to let you sabotage my reputation!"

Janty got the message. He acted wisely, and I was impressed by his response. He and his allies moved off en masse like a flock of swans, as if nothing had happened. But my feelings for Janty flared up like never before.

A mixture of emotions dominated my heart. It must have been my feminine instinct: I couldn't resist a man standing up to defend me. I also respected him for suppressing his anger and acting calmly at my request. But I also felt an acute sense of guilt at being the cause of his injuries, and I felt a stab of pain inside when I heard him groan from the pain searing through his body.

I couldn't exactly leave him in that state, so I found myself accompanying him to the empty apartment without thinking twice. My only thought was that I should stay at his side and help dress his wounds. He had a split lip, a nosebleed, and bruises all over his body.

Back at the apartment, I started to daub his wounds with cotton wool. My tears fell, mingling with his blood in the first meeting of our bodies. The white cotton wool was stained with the red of his blood, just as I was stained with a strong desire to hug him and squeeze him tight. He reached his hand up to touch my fingertips as they dabbed his lip. He stopped my fingers, then his lips began to kiss them: one kiss, then another, then another.

I moved my hand towards his cheek, away from his kisses. I longed for them to continue but I didn't want them to be restricted to my hand—other parts of me deserved them more. I hugged him tightly, then lifted his head to look in his eyes.

This was a fleeting moment of restraint, before our lips came together in a longed for embrace. The hellish pain of his injuries was soon forgotten as we were swept up to a place of such heavenly bliss I'll never forget.

ALI

When it comes to religion, we all start off barefoot and make our own shoes to fit

I knew that the path I was setting out on was full of challenges, but I had no choice other than to finish what I started: my fear of the future swept me along like a raging torrent of water. I made my decision and I had to face up to the challenges. I placed myself in God's hands and prayed to him to help me, to lighten the burden on my shoulders, for I suffer every day for the sin I have committed. The time had come to put an end to it.

I began this road with a challenge so tough I didn't know if I could overcome it. I knew I would have to stab myself in the heart, and tear out the heart of the most precious person in my life: my friend and lover, Samir.

I have always been amazed at people's ability to hurt the ones they love, and here I was preparing to hurt the kindest and most irreproachable person I have ever known, someone who has known me like no one else, who has loved me through good times and bad. I would rather die than hurt such a person, but there was no other way. I needed to tell him what I'd decided.

But in the end I couldn't quite bring myself to do it as I planned, so I let things take their normal course: for privacy, we met in a hotel room as we tend to now and again. He came up to me and hugged me the moment I closed the door. I held him tight and choked back my tears—it wasn't time for that yet. He told me how much he missed me and cursed the fact that we could only snatch the occasional brief moment together.

I let myself be guided by fate. I let myself betray him for the first time in my life. I knew that I was enjoying his body for the last time, but I denied him the right to that knowledge. I didn't know which of us was better off? Me, because I was aware of the impending catastrophe and could savor these last few moments, or him, because he was ignorant of what was coming and could enjoy our time together without anxiety or awkwardness? I let him enjoy it, and I let myself savor the moment…

Our bodies trembled in rapture and we fell back into each other's arms in an embrace of pure love. After our passion, we lay together in a state of tenderness and warmth; my head on his chest, my fingers stroking his hair, we drifted off to the symphony of physical and spiritual gratification. Our bodies lay still, silent and motionless in awe of the moment. But a few minutes were enough for my tormented soul to awaken, and I found myself pronouncing those fateful words that would forever bring an end to the most beautiful days and moments of my life.

"Samir," I said. "I'm getting married."

Samir couldn't comprehend the words he heard. I think he thought I was delirious. Maybe I was delirious. I was lost in a whirlwind of right and wrong, truth and deception.

How could I expect him to understand a decision like this, which I knew very well must seem ridiculous? Ever since we met, he has continually tried to convince me that it's our human right to love whomever we choose to love, even if it is someone of the same sex.

I've never been truly convinced. The feeling of guilt has clung to me since childhood, since I first realised that my attraction towards men was sexual. I spent my teenage years in self-denial. I used to force myself to picture a woman in my mind whenever I needed to discharge my sexual energy in masturbation. I would reach down and clutch my dick, close my eyes and imagine myself in the presence of a woman's body. My desire would collapse. I wouldn't feel anything, but would keep on rubbing. The image in my mind would switch from one woman to another, and another, and then when it finally settled on the image of a man, my desire would be restored, until he made me fall back in rapture and remorse.

I would curse myself and promise never to repeat what had happened. I would refrain from this secret habit for a few days, or sometimes for months, but my arousal always came back in the form of a dream that haunted me almost daily. This dream had me in the arms of another man, drawn in perfect detail in my mind's eye, filling me with a flood of emotions, many times more potent than anything I could summon up when I was conscious. It left me wet and squalid. Sometimes in the middle of the night, but more often at dawn, as the sun was rising, I would sheepishly sneak to the bathroom to take a cool shower and change my underwear.

I turned to prayer and fasting, persuading myself that my feelings were just a test from God and that they would fade with time and disappear altogether. I heard about cases that sounded similar to how I was feeling and strongly resisted my mind's successive attempts to make the link between all the words I was hearing. They were all negative. I'd hear some of them being shouted by the kids in the neighborhood, when they were teasing each other and throwing insults about: *queer, fag, poof.* Some were more neutral, like *gay*, and then there were the foreign-sounding terms, with more of an exotic tinge to them, words I'd read in magazines and newspapers, like *homosexual* or *sodomist.*

Which one was me? I had no idea. Did all those terms refer to the same thing? Were all the degrading words teaming up to point at me and laugh? What had I done to get branded by these names before I even knew what sex was?

I was afflicted with a raging internal conflict for many years. Some days I convinced myself that all those words and terms had nothing to do with me. They were usually aimed at men who were feminine or soft, and there was nothing feminine about me. I was proud of my manliness and would do everything I could to flaunt it. I reached puberty before most of the boys my age. My facial hair was thick and it grew densely on my chest, covering part of my back and shoulders, too. I was soon taller than most men I knew. My voice grew deep and coarse, giving me more clout than I deserved at my age. I was a very masculine-looking man in a society that reveres machismo, but that wasn't the full picture.

It was impossible to make a link between me and the prevailing belief of what a gay man is: a soft, effeminate man. That was the main argument I used when I tried to convince myself none of those names applied to me. I can't be gay, I'd tell myself. But the argument was futile. It caved in with time and with my need to understand and make sense of myself.

Deep down I knew there was a thread that linked all of those names in some way, and that it was sexual attraction towards the same sex. And my feelings were confirmed when I started researching online and I read about the scientific concept of sexual orientation. It was at a time when the Arabs lagged behind and there was an almost complete vacuum of Arabic content on the Internet, so it was much easier to find information about sexual orientation in English than it was in Arabic. It was a relatively recent concept in the Middle East, and there was no interest in Arab culture in importing this knowledge at a time when sex was generally a taboo subject, not to mention our sensitivity about the West and the moral prejudice surrounding it.

The picture began to crystallise the more I read. I was relieved when I read that the American Psychiatric Association considered same-sex sexual orientation to be normal and not a psychiatric illness that required treatment. But I was also disappointed when I read that sexual preferences are constant and don't change with time.

Initially, I wasn't convinced by what I read. I started going to see a psychotherapist as soon as I was earning enough money to have anything left over after supporting my family. I was absolutely terrified about admitting to my feelings for the first time outside my own head. Saying it out loud turned it into a certainty, a fact, a reality I had to deal with.

The therapist disagreed with everything I had read online regarding the scientific explanations for sexual orientation. He destroyed the psychological comfort I had built up from the knowledge that it wasn't a psychiatric illness and instead convinced me that I did need treatment, which he could provide. In a way, that generated a flicker of hope in me: hope that I might still live a normal life without fear or guilt about sinning against the will of God.

He asked me to take a blood test and then put me under his state-of-the-art brain-scanning machine in his clinic. He then told me that, from a physiological point of view, my brain was perfectly healthy, but that I needed long-term psychological treatment. He prescribed me an antidepressant, although I wasn't depressed at the time. He claimed that the medication would help him break the resistance within me and that within a few therapy sessions he would rid me of my sexual perversion.

So I embarked on this journey of treatment, determined to accomplish the task. Each session set me back a large sum of money, but I didn't care about the cost back then. The key thing for me was to focus and do whatever the therapist said, to rid myself of my deviant sexuality, as was my dream. He asked me if I had ever practiced homosexual acts. I could answer truthfully, at the time, that I hadn't. He compared homosexuality to an addiction and said that today I might only want to touch the hand of another man, but with the time I would want to kiss a man, and then that wouldn't be enough, and I would need more and more. Just like a smoker, it starts with smoking just one cigarette, and it ends up with you chain-smoking your way through several packs a day.

After ten sessions of therapy, I was feeling only frustration. To start with, the antidepressants added a strange tingle of joy to my life, something I'd never felt before. I was feeling good and wasn't worried about what our sessions were delving into.

He tried to take me back to my childhood, to uncover the events which he believed must have been the cause of my sexual tendencies. He asked if I had been the victim of sexual abuse. I hadn't. Well, he dodged that answer and kept coming back to it again and again, insisting that I go over every single childhood relationship with him, in case there was something I had forgotten to mention which might lead him to the source of the problem. He clearly didn't like my responses because he was convinced that the main cause of homosexuality was being subject to sexual abuse in childhood. That simply didn't apply to me.

When he realised his sexual abuse theory wasn't going anywhere, he turned to the absent-father theory. He was helped here by the fact that I really had lost my father in the Iran-Iraq war, when I was a child. He claimed that at a key moment in my psychological development, I lacked a male role model, and that was why I was attracted to men. It was just my mind trying to compensate for what I had been deprived of in my childhood. This explanation seemed fairly logical to me, initially, but as the therapy sessions dragged on without any obvious impact, doubts began to creep into my mind.

At that time, I was starting to get to know other gay men, and I started trying to make a link between his theories and their lives. Yes, some of them had lost their parents in childhood, either because of war or for other reasons, and yes, there were some who'd been victims of sexual abuse, but there were also plenty who didn't fall into either of those categories. I went back to do more research and read that there was no real relationship between being sexually abused and homosexuality, nor was there any proven link with not having a father.

Around that time, I got to know a gay journalist, an American, who was in Iraq covering the bloody massacres after the fall of Saddam. Michael was shocked when he heard about the way my therapist was trying to cure me of my sexual tendencies. He was furious about the drugs he'd put me on and warned me they could seriously upset the chemical balance in my brain.

"If that therapist was in the US, they would have withdrawn his license," Michael told me, adding that he was following an outdated treatment method which had been proven not to work. He said my therapist was exposing me to harm so that he could keep earning the money I was paying for each session, and he warned me that I could get addicted to the antidepressants and they could affect my sexual performance. Homosexuality was a perfectly normal sexual tendency, he said, and I had to learn to accept myself and live with it. I felt so humiliated when I realised!

What right did this doctor have to break someone's confidence in himself and in his body? Was he exploiting me, knowing I was weak? Or because he knew no one would hold him to account? How would I ever be able to trust another doctor after I'd been exploited in such an awful way?

How many doctors must there be out there, taking advantage of their patients for financial gain like this? How long are our doctors going to carry on rejecting scientific progress on moral grounds? And yet how can we be sure that science is right? Should we not take our religious texts and the interpretations of them as our sole source of guidance?

I wanted to stop the sessions, but he insisted I carry on until we were done. He threatened to expose me to my family if I didn't complete his course of treatment. He presented his logic wrapped up in religion, claiming that his conscience wouldn't allow him to let me do what angered God.

So I played along with his game and told him I was feeling better and that I no longer felt any desire towards men. It was the only way I could escape from his grip. I forced myself to smile, as I thanked him for curing me! As I left his clinic, I cursed that degree certificate hanging on the wall that granted so-called experts like him the right to control other people's lives.

I left all of that behind me, but the feeling of guilt still lingers to this day. I'm no longer interested in how homosexuality is classified in scientific terms. The only thing that matters now is how God sees homosexuality, and therefore I've never felt comfortable with it, even after I fell in love with another man. Sometimes I try not to think about it, because we are all 'destined for the fire,' after all; and I know Allah is forgiving, merciful, and just, and he knows me better than anyone. It is easy to judge me, but if you aren't attracted to the same sex, you have no idea how bitter it feels to be on the wrong side of the taboo.

I try to make up for my sin through prayer and fasting. I refrain from sex during Ramadan. Samir finds it odd, but he respects my wishes. Sometimes he criticises me because I don't observe every single religious rule and he thinks you can't just pick and choose bits of a religion. I agree with him, but I also know that there is no human being alive who is capable of following every religious teaching to the letter. Everyone gives what he can.

It's not as if I'm the only one who strays from the path in some respects: we all disobey in one way or another. I have one friend who fasts but doesn't pray, and who drinks alcohol but doesn't eat pork. Another friend of mine prays and fasts, and doesn't drink alcohol or eat pork, but he did have sex before he got married. Everyone has a weakness and the devil knows how to play on it. When it comes to religion, we all start off barefoot and have to make our own shoes to fit. And inevitably we criticise and condemn how other people make theirs.

But, today, I've set off on the path that society wants me to follow. It's not just for religious reasons, but also to please those around me, to please a society that disapproves of a man being a bachelor at my age. I want to please my mum and make her dream of seeing me get married come true. And I want to banish my fear of a merciless future as a middle-aged bachelor, all alone with no family, no children. I think that's what scares me the most. I find the thought absolutely terrifying.

***

Samir was stunned, lost for words.

"Well, good luck to you," he said finally, as he got up and walked out of the room without another word. I was left feeling as if I had stabbed myself in my heart.

HAYAT

Did my father take my virginity?

HE went into his room and closed the door behind him. He hadn't uttered a single word the rest of the way home. He seemed as shocked as I was by what he had done. I was shaking violently, as if delirious with fever.

The first thing I did was head to the bathroom. I felt disgusting, as if I was soiled by all the dirt in the world. His hideous smell hovered on me, smothered me, and made me feel sick.

I stripped off and stepped under a cold shower to scrub away every trace of him. My trembling body, beneath the bracing water, tried to shiver him off me, but his presence clung to me, like a demon that had invaded my body.

I scrubbed furiously with a rough sponge, trying to scratch out every hint of him from my pores. I rubbed the same patch over and over, until my skin was red. New scratches appeared on my body, adding to those I'd got from him, new wounds which felt different. I needed the pain to cover up the other scratches, to rub out the hideous memories engraved in them. The water ran red with blood. The two streams mingled, the redness of the blood winning out over the clear, transparent water.

This was a demon painting a picture of hell and I was his protagonist. He was adding the final touches to his landscape, his demonic version of existence that I struggled to comprehend. I heard him cackle wickedly as blood dripped from between my thighs. His masterpiece was complete and his maniacal laughter rang out as he dropped a thought into my mind, a question that I did not have the strength to bear.

Did my father take my virginity? The question crept across my mind, spreading a sense of horror that exceeded even everything I had been through that night. I banged my head against the wall with all my strength, again and again, trying to chase away this question. Just the thought of it was enough to drive me out of my mind. A bloodcurdling wail emerged from my throat, as I beat my fists against the bathroom wall.

"No, Dad! Nooooo!" For a moment I felt dizzy; I almost fainted. But then another voice emerged within me and, taking hold of the reins, it cursed that question and shoved it out of my mind. It flung that thought into the dark corner they call 'the subconscious' and threw away the key. I shuddered at even glancing at that sinister place where all the pain of the past few years was buried. This was a familiar voice breaking through, a steady companion that has appeared in the darkest of times, helping me bury certain events in my life. I have to make the best of a past littered with black holes so that I can keep on trudging forwards.

After my shower, I piled on my clothes, as though hiding my body under as many layers as possible, far from my father's reach. I wanted to bury my body and with it any sensation; I didn't want to feel anything. I did not want a body, I did not want any flesh, I did not want any blood. I got into my bed and buried myself under yet another layer. Let it envelope me and take me away from this world. I tried to sleep, but sleep kept evading me.

This wasn't the first time my buried fears, my demons, had emerged at this time of the night, but this time, as they flashed their teeth at me, they were starker and more gruesome than ever before. And again that dreaded question rang out, more clearly pronounced this time.

Did my father take my virginity?

I couldn't ignore it, and yet I didn't have the strength to bear it, to face the answer. So I resolved to cut my demons off in their tracks and create a new reality where my doubts *could* be buried away. There was only one way to get round this, I told myself. I would not allow my virginity to be stolen by my father, no matter what demonic voices tried to taunt me.

Let Qais come to my rescue: I'll give him my virginity to preserve what's left of my sanity.

I reached for my mobile on the bedside table. My fingers typed a text message, the words of my salvation:

Qais, get us a hotel room tomorrow. I'm ready for everything you want of me…

PART FOUR

LEILA

A sacred chant, the most cherished word in the human lexicon

LIFE is full of surprises. One minute you're stuck in a dead end, then out of the blue, you win the jackpot and you're lifted up into a beautiful dream.

Ever since Ali asked me to marry him, I've been floating about in this strange, blissful dream-like state that has lifted all my woes from my shoulders and left me without a care in the world. All of a sudden I have everything I want from my life, as if I've achieved everything that I'm supposed to achieve. I instantly forgot the exhaustion of all those years slaving away at university and all the hard work I put in to get a distinction and prove my worth to everyone. None of that matters anymore; it's like everything around me is just blossoms and rose petals. Who cares about a degree? Soon I'll have the most prestigious certificate I can ever achieve: a marriage certificate.

I still feel a bit like a princess about to be crowned queen, sitting back in my throne and looking forward to a happier future. People have started calling me '*aroos*,' the bride, a lovely nickname that will stay with me for months: I was an '*aroos*' even before our engagement party, and that's what I'll be called for the duration of our engagement and for a while after our wedding, too.

Aroos—what joy is crammed into those five letters! The name resonates in my ears like a sacred chant, the most cherished word in the human lexicon since time immemorial. Mankind has celebrated the concept of the bride throughout the history of civilisation, and countless traditions, customs, and fables have been built up around it. Contemporary Amman society is no different. We have this rich cultural heritage framed around our instinctive reverence for the miracle of procreation.

So I'm an *aroos*! I can't help but feel a rush of pride at pulling off my role in society so smoothly. I got a distinction in my degree, found a respectable job, and now I can hold my head up high as I walk with my fiancé, a man endowed with qualities that very few men possess. Good-looking, kind, and gentle-mannered, he's very well educated and hails from one of the biggest and most noble Iraqi families. Ali! His name echoes round and round in my head like a beautiful melody. Oh my gosh, I'm so in love!

He treats me with a tenderness I've never known in any man. He's quiet in nature and mild-tempered; the gentle way he speaks to me makes me feel more and more attracted to him. I always feel relaxed in his presence, and I'm so excited about the day when I can finally throw myself into his arms and enjoy that truly feminine feeling in his protective embrace. I love the dark tone of his skin and his thick, strong arms. When I see them move I can't help but imagine myself being held in them. Just his presence fills me with this exhilaration I've never felt before—something I seemed entitled to for the first time in my life. This strange happy feeling has been sizzling away inside me constantly. It bubbled up especially in the days leading up to the announcement of our engagement, when I couldn't sleep for excitement—something else I've either never felt before or never noticed, anyway.

One night I lay my head back on the pillow and just smiled. These days my smile stays on all night—like a reflection of the crescent moon in the sky, as Salma put it. Teasing me, she lay down and pulled such a big grin that we both fell about giggling. She closed her eyes, her smile still plastered across her face, and tossed her head from side to side mimicking how I've been fidgeting in bed, too restless to sleep. I was in fits of laughter.

"Salma, my lovely!" I exclaimed, getting up to give her a huge hug.

"I'm going to miss you so much, Leila," she said. "I'm going to be all on my own."

Tears welled up in my eyes as I realised how much I was going to miss her too—more than anyone, more than my mum or dad. We've shared this bedroom for as long as I can remember. And even though we haven't always been the best of friends, we're always there for each other and we always will be.

When I was little, I used to follow her around everywhere, oblivious to the fact that at that age she wanted to play with her own friends, not with me. But as we grew up, with the passing years we became closer and we started to share friends, as well as sharing aspirations and worries. These days, she stands by me through thick and thin, and she's helping me with everything to do with the wedding.

Anyway, at least my excitement stopped me from feeling anxious about the engagement party when our families met for the first time. Although it was all a bit nerve-racking, I was actually really looking forward to meeting Ali's mum and getting to know his two sisters. We arranged it for when Ali's uncle was over from Baghdad.

It all happened as per tradition, and once again I was the focus of conversation, bouncing about from one side to the other. But this time I didn't feel so much like a tennis ball being volleyed back and forth; I was more like a butterfly hovering over a field in bloom, flitting from one flower to another, dancing happily against the background of the musical hum of conversation. Nothing—not even my mum's tall tales, her often entirely fictitious accounts of my unparalleled household skills, and his mum's boasting about his family's prestigious social standing—nothing could spoil my mood that day.

***

Still getting to grips with my new status as a fiancée, I've been swept away by the thrill of reorganising my life with Ali as its axis. I admit I've had my head in the clouds and haven't paid much attention to my friends lately. I don't know whether it was being busy with planning the engagement party and wedding, and getting things ready for our house, but I've certainly noticed a distance growing between us. Perhaps it's just the realisation, subconsciously, that my social role has changed, so that all of a sudden I have much less in common with my unmarried friends. Almost overnight, our interests and outlooks have drifted irretrievably far apart.

The time I spend with Hayat and Rana has dwindled rapidly, going from seeing them at least twice a week to a couple of times a month or less. Early on, we at least spoke on the phone quite a lot, and I'd tell them about Ali and our wedding preparations, our conversations always ending with apologies for not finding time to meet up and with promises to make a date to see each other soon.

But as the months of our engagement have gone by, the phone calls have become less frequent and our meetings have dried up. Our rare chats on the phone these days are awkward and brisk, little more than an obligatory nod to the years of our friendship. So I was surprised when Hayat rang me up out of the blue, a week before the wedding, and told me she needed to meet me urgently.

"There's something really important you need to know about Ali," she said. "I can't tell you on the phone. I need to see you."

Her call left my head spinning, more annoyed than worried. What was so important that it couldn't wait until after the wedding? Why was she so insistent on meeting up now? Why couldn't she just tell me on the phone and put me at ease?

"What *is* it with you girls?" I muttered to myself. I sighed and tried to put it out of my mind, telling myself she was probably just jealous.

Rana

Within me, a new woman was born...

EVERY time I saw Janty after that night, I was plagued by an intense desire to kiss him. That first kiss made such an impact on me that for days afterwards I couldn't get it out of my head. I went over it again and again from every perspective, trying to make sense of the meaning it conveyed: the psychological dimension, the personal meaning, and the social consequences. That kiss changed me; I was no longer the person I was before.

Even if I could look at it all from the assumption that I had the right to kiss whomever I liked, I still had to try and read Janty's mind and work out how much the kiss had changed what he thought of me. Did he still respect me? Did he still feel the same way about me? I found myself plunged into completely new social territory. One kiss was enough to subtly and ever so slightly change the way I saw myself; it opened my eyes to social constraints, the intricacies and scale of which I had previously been completely unaware. After just one kiss, I found myself seized by an incredibly strong desire which was clearly at odds with my place in society as a woman, and with the moral assumptions I suppose I have built up in recent years, after all.

My thoughts were suddenly dominated by handed-down traditions, society's moral heritage, and above all the idea that a man will lose all respect for a woman if she gives him a taste of her body before marriage. I became touchy around Janty, watching his every move and obsessively analysing everything he said to me. I was desperate for a sign from him to reassure me that nothing had changed and that his feelings for me remained the same.

But Janty was on another page altogether. He was upset by my touchiness, which he interpreted as me losing confidence in him, and he took it as an insult that I had pigeonholed him according to an outdated way of thinking that he refused to succumb to.

"Don't you trust me? Why have you changed towards me? Why do you suddenly think I'm some bastard who's going to mess you around?"

Janty told me that it was my bold character he'd found attractive, and the fact that I wasn't like the other girls. He liked me all the more the day I bit the bullet and made the first move on the pretext of wanting to copy his notes from the lecture. He liked my spontaneity and my some-times over-enthusiastic responses to things. And he loved my daring choice of clothes, my short hair, and the way I dyed it red.

"The first thing I noticed about you was your short hair. I knew straight away that you're not like all the other girls. So why are you being like them now?"

Janty's words were hugely reassuring and filled me with a sense of confidence in myself that I wasn't used to. This feeling, coupled with my innate love of breaking the rules, helped me decide I was ready to move from our first kiss to our second, then our third, and then onto other things which introduced me to my body as a woman. After refusing for all this time, I still needed weeks and even months to break down the psychological barriers around my body. I was haunted by feelings of remorse after every intimate moment we spent together, and I'd go back and withdraw into my shell, and keep my distance from Janty for a while. We'd go several days without meeting up, and then, gradually, the desire would return, even more strongly than before, and then I'd find myself taking the plunge and asking to see him again.

The more I started to fall for him, and the more we saw of each other, the more the physical dimension become an essential part of the dynamics between us. I felt a sense of intimacy in his arms that I'd never experienced before. When our bodies came together it was enough to dissolve any tension between us from an argument or a disagreement over some trivial little thing. The tension would also grow as the time passed since our last date, and I'd find myself unable to wait until I could be close to him again, desperate for our bodies to melt together and for all those petty worries to be washed away.

I guess it's normal to feel anxious when faced with something unfamiliar, but it's amazing how quickly we adapt. We instinctively paint the unfamiliar with a gloss of familiarity, so we can flip our anxiety on its head and find peace of mind instead. Well, that seemed to be how my fear of going to Janty's apartment gave way to a feeling of being completely relaxed there. Going there started to seem a completely normal thing to do. I no longer thought it strange like before; I would just open the door and go in, as if I were at home opening my own front door. In the same way, my fear of physical contact between us diminished and my psychological defences caved in, yielding to the part of me that knew pleasure and no longer felt any need of fear.

My virginity was a red line that we tacitly agreed we would respect, without ever saying so much in words. We managed to steer clear of trouble for a good few months, until even this taboo collapsed under the pressure of our intense thirst which could be quenched only by breaking the rules. And that was when, on one night of madness, we allowed our bodies to wallow in the balmy sea of desire.

A year had passed since we first got to know each other and we decided to celebrate our anniversary. As a surprise for me, Janty prepared a candle-lit dinner at his apartment, creating a magical romantic atmosphere the likes of which I'd only ever seen in Hollywood movies and soap operas: soft lighting, candles flickering, music playing quietly in the background. Our favourite song, Wael Kfoury's "If Our Love's a Mistake (*Law Hobna Ghalta*)," came on the iPod and it felt like he was singing it especially for us, as if we were telling the world to leave us in peace, even if everyone saw our love as a mistake.

Janty had cooked dinner and set the table. For ages he had been promising me he would cook me his favourite Circassian dish, *shipsu pasta*.

"Ah, so this is *shipsu pasta*! Finally I get to try it!"

"Yes, darling, this is it! Go on then, *habibti*, try some. What do you think?"

"And you've even got us a bottle of wine?"

"So we can celebrate in style, *habibti*."

That night was one of the most wonderful nights of my life. A beautiful, happy night I'll never forget. We retired to the sofa after we'd eaten. I lay back in his arms. It had been a month since the last time we'd been alone like this and I couldn't wait to kiss him. Little kisses at first were followed by longer kisses, fuelling our desire.

He carried me to the bedroom. His arms around me, he laid me down beneath him. His forehead pressed against mine; he seized control of my lips. I was captive to a body that I so desired, captive to a desire that possessed all of me.

I don't know if it was desire, or passion, or an urgent need. I don't know if it was a snap decision or something I knew I wanted to happen. I don't know if it was the alcohol or if it was our love alone that took us to that point. But at that moment, those red lines lost all significance. They crumbled in the path of my desire to bring him joy, and to feel every bit of him as a man, and to feel every bit the woman I was. That was the day the woman inside me blossomed, the day I became truly whole.

"I'm ready," I whispered in his ear. He was also ready. And, silently, our bodies were entwined more intimately than ever before. I felt pain mixed with desire... and within me a new woman was born.

SALMA

There is no longer any joy in this world.

THERE seems to be a fashion at the moment in the newspapers for features about abandoned babies. Every day I read another story about a newborn baby found abandoned at the door of a mosque, dumped out with the trash, or even left under Abdoun Bridge. Strangely, these stories seem to have proliferated recently and everyone's wondering what's causing this phenomenon, and why it has snowballed to an extent we've never seen before.

It's a major topic of conversation, filling column inches in the papers, and it's everywhere on social media; everyone has their own theory about the root of this phenomenon. Some point the finger at the economic crisis which is pushing single mothers to abandon their children because they can't afford to feed them. Others think it stems from the moral decay in society since the country opened up to the West, with foreign TV channels, the Internet, and mobile phones all spreading their evil influence.

Some writers see a link with honour crimes, with families being afraid of disgrace and girls being terrified they'll be killed if anyone finds out they got pregnant outside the sanctity of marriage. Others suggest it is simply a trend in the reporting: that the news coverage has increased because people's interest in it has increased, although it has always existed as a phenomenon in society and always will. The only thing that's new is journalists seeing it as a sensation that sells, and that's why they care about it all of a sudden— and are increasing their coverage.

As for me, I see Yasmine in every story I read, and all I want to do is gather up all the abandoned babies and deliver them back to the loving embrace of their mothers. Sometimes I find myself daydreaming, and picture myself walking through the streets of Amman, searching the bins for an infant whose wailing cry echoes in my heart. I'm ripped to pieces at the sound, and I rush to pick up the child and rock him in my arms. As the baby's features become clear, I see it is a little girl, Yasmine. I take her home, locking the door behind me. I hear a commotion outside, shouting and fists banging on the door. A group of men force their way in and seize her from my arms, telling me she should be in an orphanage and that I, a single woman, have no right to look after a child, no matter how much love and compassion I have to offer.

A few days ago, one particular news article made me stop and think. In it, someone from the Ministry of Social Development said that while most applications to foster a child come from families, there is nothing in the law to stop an individual from being given the right to foster. Two Jordanian women had recently succeeded in gaining the right to foster a child.

The idea made me feel dizzy. I couldn't help wondering, was that something I could do? If fate didn't bless me with a husband, would it be possible for me to apply to foster a child on my own? Would my circumstances allow it? Who would stand by me? Would my mum support me? Is there any way on earth I could get my father to agree?

'No' would seem to be the only logical answer to all of these questions. I'm quite sure they would all say I was mad and laugh at me, and if I went ahead and did it anyway, then most likely they would throw me out and do everything they could to stand in my way.

My future looks pitch black to me. I'm destined to end up all alone in my father's house, a prisoner to social constraints for the rest of my life. And after a long life, my father will move on to the next realm and my refuge will become my brother's house, under his wife's merciless thumb and watchful eye.

My life no longer has any flavour to it, with only fear of the future filling my heart. I am constantly stabbed by people's looks, their whispers, by the feeling that I'm a failure. I have nothing but melancholy inside me and I struggle to see any joy in this world. One dismal day follows another. Whether they pass slowly or quickly, I barely notice, but they pass without flavour or scent or colour.

All my friends have drifted away from me after getting married. They're busy these days with their houses and their husbands and their children. Even Leila is preoccupied with her fiancé and the wedding preparations. Although she's trying to involve me, I feel like she's already become distant from me as now she has her own things to do and worry about.

My mum has ratcheted up the pressure on me after the relief of getting Leila paired off. I am now the only thing left that troubles her and matchmaking me is her one remaining goal in life. She's been setting up opportunities for me to meet men who are looking for a bride, men she finds through her friends. She forces me to meet them and give them a chance, even though I don't feel the slightest whiff of attraction, not on any level—physical, intellectual, or spiritual.

She can never see anything wrong with any of the men who show an interest in me. Anything that might be wrong with a man pales in comparison with the disgrace and horror of being a spinster. There's no shame in a man being ugly. If he's obese, there's no shame in that either. If he's old, it's fine. If the words that come out of his mouth are coarse and vulgar, that's fine too. Even the old saying 'the only thing a man should be ashamed of is his bank balance' is not true in my mother's eyes.

I hear the same old record playing day in, day out. She accuses me of being arrogant and of burying my head in the sand. She warns me I'll regret it in the future, that whatever I find unacceptable now will be desirable in a few years, and that a girl's worth is inversely proportional to her age—she loses value with each passing year. Then she pours fuel on the fire by constantly reminding me of all the horrible situations I've been in.

"Remember Nasreen's wedding? She put you on the kids' table because you were the only single girl she'd invited. Remember when your car tyre got a puncture and our neighbor came and helped you, the guy who'd just got married? Remember how his new bride came out and laid into you? Remember Eid last year, how all the girls in the family came with all their husbands and fiancés and you felt all alone?"

Yes, I remember. And being made to dwell on all those situations hurts, Mum! It makes me even more depressed than usual, and my mum seems to delight in harping on about it, picking open the wounds, so she can persuade me to accept whoever comes my way. She wants to see me as a bride at any cost. Everyone wants to see me as a bride at any cost. And I want to be a bride, too—but *not* at any cost.

I don't know what planted this crazy notion in my head. I don't know how the seed germinated and grew and started to take over my mind. Perhaps it's the wretched mood I'm in? Perhaps it's the instinct to run away from a reality I can no longer face?

I feel like I'm being shackled, like I'm paralysed. I can't move for the hands throttling my neck. Hands stretching from all sides to cut off the blood from my heart. I want to scream, to shake them off. I want to run, as far as I can get from this world. I no longer feel anything but arrows stabbing me, wounds exacerbated by the clawing hands of my family.

They want me to be a bride… okay, so I'll be a bride. On Leila's wedding day, there won't be just one celebration, there'll be two. Two weddings, two brides, two celebrations: Salma and Leila—both brides on one night. How happy you'll be, Mum! I'll finally make all your dreams come true, all on one day!

HAYAT

The spectre of my father loomed over me

I felt like I was betraying my father as I lay in Qais's arms, in the hotel room that day. It was as if I was punishing him for what he had done, as if revenge was what I was looking for. I needed a response to what he had done to me: I needed to give myself to another man, someone to take his place and to pull me away.

But the memories flashed through my mind as Qais ravished my body. Qais wasn't the only one there with me: the spectre of my father loomed over me. His voice echoed in my ears. No sooner had Qais's fingertips touched my breasts, than an image came to me of myself as a young, innocent girl, sitting on the floor of the lounge, surrounded by paper and coloured pens. My father called over to me: "Hayat!" He sat me down on his lap. He picked up a pen and drew a naked female body next to the butterflies I had drawn. He traced over the drawing, emphasising the features, and wrote 'Hayat' next to it. Next to Hayat, he drew a man with a moustache. He hugged me tight and planted a kiss on my forehead, then ran his fingers across parts of me which he warned me never to share with anyone else. He called me his princess, saying that I was so beautiful that I must never allow anyone else to touch me besides him.

His words were set in stone as the law for a young girl whose eyes were opening up to the world in her father's arms. He dictated principles and morals to me which he formulated at a whim to suit him. He wrote the rules for an illicit relationship which no one dared admit even existed. He exploited his role as a father to derive pleasure from a young girl who didn't know better, a girl who looked to him as the only man in her life, the source of her sense of security and confidence, the axis around which her world rotated.

That girl was now in the arms of another man. She wanted to wipe out all memory of her body, so scarred and sullied with grime and the stench of one man. That girl has grown up to realise that the nearest people to her failed to provide the most basic protection human beings can extend to one another. That girl has grown up to realise that the person who was granted the most trust in the world was the same person who betrayed her most severely.

That night with Qais was not enough to silence the screams in my heart or to erase the tortured memories. I found myself asking Qais for sex again and again in the following days as if I no longer knew how to live without it. Like morphine, it numbed the pain and gave me just a morsel of psychological gratification knowing that my body no longer belonged to my father. Day after day I decided to offer myself to another man for his enjoyment; who can say if he deserved it?

It wasn't long, though, before Qais was out of the picture. He claimed he was feeling guilty for neglecting his family, and that his moral principles told him he should give his marriage another chance and try to salvage what was left of his relationship with his wife. Yet another betrayal from the man who had stolen my heart. He left me feeling lost and alone. All I could do was look for another man to fill the gap he had left in my life, to somehow extinguish this physical need.

And yet after Qais, life changed. Hayat changed. She was no longer burdened by restrictions on the nature of her relations with men. There was no longer anything to shy away from. She already knew the past she would have to bear.

This was a young woman swamped with secrets she had to conceal from those around her in order to maintain her social ties. But she was now aware of the special liaisons she could form with the opposite sex, and under the cover of secrecy required by both parties, she started to set up the circumstances for a series of one-night stands to satisfy the desire that plagued her—part pleasure, part pain.

Few men in Amman are deterred by the social norms that are such a burden on women. If a girl desires something that is forbidden to her gender, even though she ought perhaps to have as much right to it as a man, she will find it readily available.

I soon found that having multiple sexual relationships, no matter how short and fleeting, opens you up to connect with other people—people who might provide work opportunities or possess knowledge that can help you progress in life. Though I had numerous sexual partners, I wouldn't exactly describe it as licentious. I never gave myself in exchange for money, and that perhaps meant I managed to retain a degree of respect.

But I didn't discourage offers of help from my bedfellows. Sometimes I would open up and talk about how I needed a job to earn a living and help my family out. It wasn't long before I met Amr, a guy in his forties who was a pilot with Royal Jordanian Airlines. I told him the lengths I was going to in looking for a decent job. And he told me how hard it was for the airline to recruit air stewardesses, because the role was still frowned on in society, and that held young women back from applying.

So I applied, and it turns out it's a job I'm perfectly qualified for. I'm the right height and weight. I'm comfortable around men and I speak English fluently. And I'm not gripped by fear for my reputation like most girls. I couldn't care less if it reduces my chances of getting married. I've always sensed that if I'm ever going to, it would probably be to a foreigner anyway, because I'm unlikely to find a single Jordanian man who would be willing to accept the past I carry on my shoulders.

After all, marriage is the furthest thing from my mind right now. All I want from a man is the pleasure that can be obtained from just one night. For a flight attendant, those opportunities would be boundless. I don't think my father will object, especially when I tell him about the seductive salary which is more than what he earns, not to mention the gifts I'll bring my family from abroad.

It suits Amr perfectly, too. He can take me with him, far

from prying eyes, far from his wife. We'll be able to enjoy each other without worrying about where to meet, without the fear of running out of time or being spotted together.

Sometimes I look in the mirror and I don't like what I see. I do what I can to justify myself when I'm plagued by guilt towards Amr's wife. I persuade myself that the world owes it to me, and that I have to protect myself first and foremost, even if it means hurting other people. I'm often amazed at our human ability to create our own logic to justify our actions, and to find a way to feel good about ourselves. I, too, have my own internal logic, and I consider it my right like anyone else.

In fact, I feel like part of my humanity has died, and that I no longer feel much sympathy towards other people. After being betrayed by one after another of the people I trusted most, I don't have much confidence left. As far as I'm concerned, human beings have proven themselves generally to be weak and contemptible. We tend to be weak until we find someone weaker than ourselves, and then we become stronger at their expense. I no longer want to be one of the victims. If I have to trample on weaker people on the way, that's what I'm going to have to do.

This is something I ask myself a lot: am I really weak inside? Or do I just seem weak to other people, which tempts them to exploit me? Is it human nature or was it written in my fate? Or is it perhaps a reflection of my relationship with my father, something that I carry with me wherever I go, making me destined to build the same relationship over and over, where I am always the weaker party?

***

Oum George could read that weakness in my eyes when I went to see her a couple of days after the incident with my father. I was lost and falling apart; I didn't know what to do. My distress was etched in my face as I set foot in her house. The second she held her arms out to me, I burst into tears. I was in desperate need of a reassuring hug, a sympathetic older friend to make me feel safe—a feeling I could barely remember.

Her living room was full of women that day. It was a religious meeting, they said, and they invited me to come and join them. They were reading and discussing verses from the Bible, and then they were going to pray together.

I didn't feel very comfortable with the idea of attending a religious study session with a group of Christian women. Ordinarily, I would do everything I could to avoid that kind of situation, but that day I didn't have the strength to resist. I urgently needed a glimmer of hope to restore something of my sanity. She read that hesitation within me, as well as sensing my need.

"Come and join us," she said, placing her hand on my shoulder. "Come and listen, and afterwards we'll talk." So I sat down with them, and listened to the discussion, but my mind was elsewhere, in my own private world.

"Hayat…" I heard someone say. "Listen to this lovely verse: 'Come to me, all you who are troubled and weighted down with care, and I will give you rest.' Matthew 28:11. The Messiah loves us all and calls us all to him to find peace."

Again and again, it seemed like the sermon was directed

at me and, unnervingly, Oum George kept picking out
verses and explaining them in such a way that they seemed
directly applicable to my situation. The conversation was
about the challenges we all face in life and how impossible
it is for man to carry his troubles alone. They talked about
our weakness as human beings and our desperate need for
Christ the Messiah to stand at our side. A couple of ladies
spoke about problems they had faced and how they had
confronted them by praying to Jesus Christ to bring peace
to their hearts and to help them in their time of great need.

Oum Fadi spoke about the hard times her family lived
through when her husband lost his job. They could no longer
make ends meet and were struggling to feed their children
without his income. She was only able to get through those
days, she said, because Christ had been at her side and had
given her strength. Her faith had wavered as she came under
all this pressure, but it returned stronger than ever when it
seemed that the hidden hand of God was reaching out to
help her.

Then there was Oum Khalil who spoke about having
cancer, and how when she was weak and feverish, the Virgin
Mary appeared to her and told her she would live to see
her grandson and that she would name him Hana after St
Johana, John the Baptist. At the time, she didn't even know
that her daughter was pregnant, and the doctors had told
her that she had only a few months left to live. Now her
daughter was six months pregnant, and Oum Khalil was
excited at the prospect of seeing her grandson before she
left this life.

These stories all seemed artificial to me, cut off from reality. I thought these women must all be deluding themselves for the sake of finding comfort at an extremely difficult time. I understood that Isa, or 'the Messiah,' the son of Mariam, was one of the prophets sent by God to show mankind the way, but I couldn't understand how the stories had mutated to such an extent that these people saw him as a living God.

Back then, I was as far as I possibly could be from any divinity, Christian or Muslim. It just left a bitter taste in my mouth when I thought of a God who hadn't intervened to save me when I was a child, and who was going to torture me in hell when I die, after I had given my virginity to Qais. Is that the just Lord that all these people believe in?

I wasn't looking for justice. All I was interested in was a feeling of safety, or perhaps a modicum of kindness. I didn't know whether or not I would be able to tell Oum George what had happened. I wasn't sure whether or not it was wise to tell her. I didn't know what her reaction would be, or what she would do. There was the risk she might tell my father, which would be the end of me—there was nothing I was more afraid of than him.

Oum George and I sat down by ourselves after the session, when all the women had gone home. She looked into my eyes and said that she could see great sadness in them. She said I was like her daughter and could share with her whatever was on my mind. To begin with, I hesitated, and made something up. I told her it was nothing, just a small problem that I would be able to deal with by myself.

But she urged me to talk and started to interrogate me bit by bit.

"Is it something to do with the family? Or is it your father? You can tell me, darling, don't be afraid."

I didn't say anything at first, but then I started to break down. My voice gave me away as I started to share my story. For a few moments I could barely speak, the words didn't have the strength to come out of my mouth.But then they did. I was struck by panic even worse than that night my father attacked me. This was the first time in my life that I had told someone what I'd endured for all those years. This was the first time I had heard my voice utter those most intimate details of what I'd suffered. My words were so tightly bound up in shame. Talking seemed to strip me bare, as my words revealed the shame at the heart of my family, a family which seemed so normal to everyone else.

My tears fell as she listened. She hugged me tightly and let my tears wet her clothes and her hair, forming a damp patch on her shoulder. I felt her tears too and heard her breath quicken in distress.

But she had nothing to say in response. She herself wasn't strong enough to support me. Her world revolved around her Messiah. Her solution, like the women at her religious gathering, was to launch into prayer on my behalf, and after going to see her a few times I sensed that her main concern was to bring me into the fold of Christianity rather than to protect me or support me.

So I decided not to see her again and to carry on my

path alone in future. Never again will I let anyone, not even Oum George, exploit me for their own ends.

PART FIVE

ALI

I play along with their game to avoid getting hurt

AFTER Samir left the hotel room that night, I had a difficult few days. I missed him more than I could bear. I couldn't imagine what my life would be like without him. At first I thought it would be better for both of us if we avoided each other. But it was only a couple of days before I started to find his absence extremely hard to bear—impossible, in fact. It was everything I could do to resist calling him, but I held out for another two days.

After four days, though, my resistance crumbled completely. I just wanted to hear his voice. I needed reassurance that he was okay. So many dark thoughts had crossed my mind, like I was trapped in a film, a thriller where in one scene after another he was always the victim. Was he okay? What if something terrible had happened to him? A car accident? What if he was ill? Did he hate me? What was he doing now? How badly had I hurt him? What if he had done something to harm himself? Or disappeared from the world altogether?

I picked up my mobile and dialled his number. My heartbeat quickened. I was agitated, impatient to hear his voice. I didn't know if he'd answer or not. I also didn't know what I would say if he did answer. I only knew that I wanted to hear his voice and to tell him how much I loved him and how much I missed him.

He didn't answer. His phone rang several times and then cut off. I tried again and then a third time. No answer. I went into my room and closed the door behind me. I burst into tears and wept like I'd never wept before in my life. I felt lost, like everything around me had lost its meaning without him. Like his absence had sucked all the colour from the world around me and life had lost its sparkle. Everything assumed a hue of black, white, or grey.

I went round to his house and I held back my tears as I knocked on the door. How could I explain myself to his mother when she let me in, if I was crying? She'd be horrified. She'd ask herself, 'Who is this man sobbing over his love for another person?' And the other person was another man: her son.

I sat in his living room, waiting for him to come home. Slowly, slowly, minutes passed by, then hours. When he finally came in, I stood up and looked into his eyes. We were both silent. We walked towards each other without either of us uttering a sound. I held him close as tears filled my eyes. I could feel his tears falling, too. For a few moments, we both whispered to each other, "Okay, that's it," and "enough." But every whisper just stirred more emotion and brought more tears. We were silent for a moment or two, until we'd both calmed down. It was only then that I managed to whisper, "I love you." That brought a smile to his face.

"Me too," he whispered. "Even more." Then he added, "You bastard."

He got changed and we went out together. In the car, I gripped onto his hand like I was afraid he might run away.

We really needed to talk. This was an impossible situation and we needed to find a way out. He absolutely refused to share me with anyone else, and he wasn't prepared to lead a life with me where he was in the shadows, constantly in second place after my family. And he certainly didn't want to be my secret lover or be complicit in deceiving someone else, an innocent person.

But I so wanted to get married and have a family, both of which would be impossible with him. I suggested that he could get married too. That way we could each have our own family, but carry on seeing each other in secret. He rejected that idea, too, saying it was hypocritical and deceptive. He said you can't correct one mistake by committing another, and that even if he wanted to have a family and children it didn't justify a lifelong marriage that was based on deception and lies.

I told him that wasn't how I saw it. I really do think married life is about more than sex. I'm determined to offer Leila everything I can in terms of comfort and security, and I plan to work hard to build the best possible life for us.

But Samir and I couldn't seem to find a middle ground. And yet splitting up seemed out of the question, especially after seeing how painful the last few days had been. I begged him to stay with me, even just until the wedding. I'm terrified about getting married—I need him by my side. He was pretty upset about it, but in the end he agreed. That was when I realised I can't let him feel like Leila is more important than he is. But at the same time, I know I need to give Leila the attention she deserves. I can't let her sense that there's someone else in my life who is more important. I can never let my guard down. I need to always be there for them, both of them, and to meet their every need.

***

Leila is great. She's easygoing and doesn't ask much of me. I see the beaming smile on her face whenever we meet, and that makes me smile too. I praise her a lot and try to make her feel like the most beautiful girl in the world, which always makes her blush. She's always telling me how happy she is and how excited she is about our life ahead and all the wonderful moments that she'll share with me.

We spend most of our time together doing up the apartment, buying stuff for it, and getting ready for the wedding. I'm trying not to cut corners. My finances are back to normal and we don't need to scrimp, so I told her not to worry about money, just to plan the wedding of her dreams.

I introduced her to Samir. I told her that he's my best friend, my closest buddy. I figured his being male would rule out any doubts she might have about our relationship. It shouldn't be too easy to read between the lines. She likes him and they've quickly become friends, in a way. She always stands by him when the three of us go out together. Nothing can save me when they team up against me, except perhaps Salma when she comes out with us. She's always on my side.

We tend to have nights out together, the four of us, at

cafés and restaurants around Amman. Leila organises everything. Samir is usually reluctant to join us and would prefer to see me on my own. So I'm constantly begging him and trying to persuade him to come, because I'm much happier and more relaxed in his company.

Occasionally we bump into some other gay friends of ours. I usually feel awkward and avoid saying hello, especially if it's a friend who's particularly camp. It's obvious from their looks and everything about them that they're clearly gay. I'm worried Leila will sense something. I don't know what I would say if she asked me how I really knew these people.

***

One day, it happened exactly as I'd feared. I suddenly bumped into Tamer, a young Egyptian guy whom I first met at a friend's house. He called my name and rushed to give me a hug. I said hello but kept it brief. I tried to keep a distance between him and Leila, to avoid having to introduce them.

I feel bad for Tamer whenever I think about what he's been through. He must really need his friends' support, so my reaction that day must have hurt. He had bleached his hair, and it was longer than before and parted on the right. He had a small earring in one ear. The strong scent of a feminine perfume wafted from him. He had face powder on, giving him a pale yet slightly shiny complexion. He held his hand out softly like some kind of aristocratic lady. He winked at me and whispered, "So, is that your fiancée? Not bad—she's quite a looker!"

I looked at him sharply, urging him to keep it down. I ended the conversation quickly and promised to give him a call in the next few days.

Tamer is a very effeminate man or, as he prefers to see himself, actually a woman. Among friends, he calls himself Nawal after the Lebanese singer Nawal al-Zoghbi, whom he adores. He knows all her songs by heart. He takes every opportunity when he's at a party with gay friends to wear women's clothes and show off his talents as an artiste.

He grew up with his parents in Saudi Arabia. He was already very effeminate as a child, and he seemed to get even more camp as he got older. He told me once about something that had happened when he was in primary school. When he reached the third year, the kids were split into two schools: one for boys and one for girls. He came home crying and asked his dad why they had put him with the boys and not the girls.

"Son, you're a boy—that's why," his father replied.

"No, Dad, I'm a girl," Tamer insisted.

The father remained quite sure that his son was a boy, while Tamer was convinced he was a girl. When he was older, his father decided to send him to university in Egypt, assuming that it was the decadent life in Saudi that had contributed to his son's feminine tendencies and that a harsher lifestyle in Egypt would turn him into the sort of man he could be proud of.

Of course, the opposite was the case, and Tamer enjoyed

a lot more freedom in Cairo, far from the watchful gaze of his father, and he soon made a lot of friends in the gay and transgender community. He started going to the Queen Boat every weekend with his friends, a nightclub on a boat on the Nile, near the Marriott Hotel. The club was well known as a place where gay men could go to dance, hang out, and meet other men.

One night the Egyptian police decided to raid the club and arrest everyone there. Tamer wasn't in the mood for going out that night and hadn't intended to go to the Queen Boat, but he gave in when his friend insisted.

As they approached the club, they noticed the police cars everywhere, but somehow they didn't appreciate the danger. They didn't realise that the police had raided the club and were arresting everyone in sight. When they got closer, it started to dawn on them what was going on.

Tamer saw his friend, a waiter at the Queen Boat, being led away by two police officers. The waiter tried to warn Tamer with his facial expression not to come any closer and to get away quick. The warning didn't work and in fact just incriminated Tamer, as the policeman on his right noticed and ran to arrest him too.

Because Tamer was so camp, there was no doubt about him being gay, unlike some of the other men, so the officer didn't think twice before insulting him and shoving him into the police van along with the others who had been arrested inside the club.

That night was a terrifying experience for Tamer: he was transferred from one police station to another with all the others, until he was finally held in one police department. That was when it really started to hit home. The interrogations started. The security services did everything they could to get the detainees to confess to gross indecency.

Dozens of men had been arrested, but within a few hours several had been released. The guys they released were the more butch-looking ones, because, the way they police saw it, being gay was associated with looking effeminate. They released some of the foreigners because they weren't the intended target of the arrest operation and also to avoid any diplomatic complications. Then they released anyone from influential families, after they were inundated with phone calls.

And finally, they released everyone who was wearing white boxer shorts, on the grounds that, in their minds, being gay was also associated with a Western influence. As Egyptian underpants are traditionally white, anyone wearing underwear of any other colour was clearly under the spell of the West and was morally depraved. Unfortunately, the boxers Tamer was wearing that night, an international brand from a new store that had just opened in Cairo a few months earlier, were green.

The police used several torture methods that night to extract confessions from the detainees, including setting the police dogs on them, whipping them with the tubes from shisha pipes, and hosing them down with cold water. To start with, Tamer refused to confess, but since childhood he'd been terrified of dogs, so when he saw them approaching he broke down and signed the confession they'd prepared for him.

A few days later, he found himself being taken to a state hospital. He was surrounded in the operating theatre by several doctors of both genders. In one of the most degrading moments of his life, Tamer was subjected to an anal examination, summarised in a report issued a few hours later with the humiliating phrase 'Used from behind.'

It was like he'd landed in some hideous nightmare. Those days he spent in prison consisted of one monstrous scene after another, completely devoid of any human justice, where men were replaced by savage monsters that revelled in torturing their victims. A dark cloud of humiliation, pain, and fear descended on his world.

Gross indecency wasn't the only charge levelled against him. He was also charged with several other crimes as part of a political conspiracy that he only became aware of later. As well as gross indecency, he was also accused of devil worship, belonging to an illegal religious group, and collaborating with the enemy Israel.

It wasn't beyond the Arab regimes to exploit moral taboos for the sake of popular legitimacy and cheap political victory. The social and moral rejection of the gay community in the Arab world made them an easy target for politicians who wanted to score points with the general public. After going to court, Tamer gradually realised how sinister and squalid all these machinations really were.

Someone who was related to a former Egyptian president had intended to run in the presidential election against

Hosni Mubarak. The family were political heavyweights, so the current government felt an urgent need to act before things got critical. The *mukhabarat* had compiled a report investigating the entire family in the hope of finding some dirt on a relative who was known for having homosexual inclinations.

Besides his sexual preferences, this person also collected pictures of himself with other men in various sexual positions. He was very creative, too, and in his imagination he had invented a kind of fictional character, a reflection of the man he longed for. Among his papers, the *mukhabarat* officers stumbled across something he'd written describing how he loved and worshipped this character like some kind of god.

It was the ideal basis for a story that would stir outrage in Egyptian society and put an end to any hope this family had of a future in politics. In people's minds, his worship of this fictitious character would be synonymous with him worshipping the devil. The sexually explicit photos were all the proof they needed to confirm the allegations against him. Homosexuality was something the Arab press tended to portray as going hand-in-hand with devil worship, and the gay community was there to complete the story as proof that such people existed, fellow adherents of this cult. But for the final nail in the coffin, they also needed to pad the story with some connection to the Zionist conspiracy to inflate it into an issue of national security, so they threw some detail about his previous visits to Israel into the mix.

Meanwhile, the Egyptian police had arrested a number

of men charged with soliciting homosexual activity on the street, a week before the raid on the Queen Boat. This operation was part of the grand plan to lump the two groups together and add prostitution to the list of charges.

Every single charge laid against Tamer was enough on its own to leave him exposed and gave the prison wardens ample pretext to treat him with contempt and aggression. His effeminate looks alone were enough to turn on one of the wardens who, like so many others, suffered from pent-up sexual frustration in the repressive Egyptian society which refused to allow any kind of relationship between the two sexes outside of the institution of marriage.

The warden started off buttering him up gently, trying to lure him into satisfying his sexual desire. When Tamer rejected these advances, the guard turned violent, beat him, and raped him. His cries echoed around the prison, bouncing off the walls of the other cells. But the guard just got more fired up and turned even more brutal.

When his father came to visit him in jail that day, Tamer didn't dare tell him what had happened. Shame held him back from admitting that he'd been raped. By the time he stood before the judge, though, he had plucked up the courage to mention it. He imagined that the judge might have a modicum of humanity in him and would stand up for justice. Tamer was almost bowled over from shock when he heard the judge's reply: "Well, take a look at yourself. Who could blame them?"

"Who could blame them?!"

Tamer realised that he lived in the most chauvinistic

society on the face of the earth, a society where femininity was seen as nothing more than the potential to turn men on and satisfy their sexual urges. It was a culture where it was the woman who was blamed for any kind of sexual liaison outside marriage, where a woman's natural expression of her femininity was seen as a free invitation to men to abuse her and treat her with contempt.

This was a reversal of roles, where the definitions of 'criminal' and 'victim' were turned on their heads. A man could be the victim of desires that were aroused by a woman's slightest gesture. She was the guilty party because his arousal was her doing; if he raped her, it was a natural response for which she alone would bear the consequences. Tamer here was no different to any other woman in the eyes of the judge, who subscribed to all these same cultural prejudices. Tamer's obvious femininity had provoked the guard to rape him, so he himself was to blame and it was he who would face punishment.

He was sentenced to a year's imprisonment during which he was subjected to every kind of abuse and humiliation imaginable, including beatings and rape. When he was released a year later, the court's ruling was overturned by the state, under pressure from international human rights organisations which argued that the first trial was unjust.

A new verdict was issued, but this time Tamer was sentenced to three years in jail from the date of the retrial. The sentence was more than he could bear after the torture he had been through, so he tried to escape from his life by committing suicide. Fortunately, he didn't succeed and a few days later an American human rights organisation managed to get him out and get him to Jordan until they could arrange for him to claim humanitarian asylum somewhere in the West.

My life seems so easy compared to his. We've both found ourselves outside of the traditional parameters of the definition of a man in our society. Being so obviously camp has meant he's had no way of hiding or blending in or pretending to play the role society expects of him. It's different for me in that my sexual preferences are less apparent. My sexuality is something private, and I appear to others as they want to see me. I play along with their game to avoid getting hurt.

That day, after talking to him, I went and sat back down in the café. On my right was my fiancée and on my left was my lover. I felt like the protagonist in a comic farce, some complex character which the playwright had endowed with an animal instinct for camouflage, a skill I'd honed not only to survive, but also to thrive, in a society that is more concerned with make-believe than with reality.

RANA

He who is without sin may cast the first stone

DIZZINESS, nausea, fatigue… sometimes I suffered from the lot, and yet at other times I didn't feel anything at all. At first I thought I must be sick. Maybe it was something I'd eaten or perhaps the flu. I ignored the symptoms, but it went on for days, then weeks.

Something strange was happening to me, something I'd never experienced before. I couldn't ignore the physical changes in my body. I seemed to be putting on weight and getting broader across the pelvis, and my stomach seemed to be swelling.

Surely I wasn't pregnant?

The idea shot across my mind like a bullet, as fast as lightning and every bit as devastating. It hit me straight in the heart and blood gushed from the wound. But I bandaged it up and managed to push the idea from my mind. I preferred to stick my head in the sand and carry on as I was. I was not ready to face an idea as terrifying as that.

Surely I couldn't have got pregnant as easily as that? Was it really that straightforward?

Yes, I'd had sex with Janty several times since that night, but we always used a condom. There was just one time when we didn't—only once. He had run out. We agreed we would be careful. We wanted to see what it was like to feel we were truly close, without the layer of rubber separating us. He promised to withdraw the moment he came, and he did, but maybe he was a fraction too late.

That fraction of a delay was enough to turn the lives of two people upside down, enough to create the life of a third person...

It's crazy how quickly everything can change. Life usually ticks by with such deadening monotony. Months and years can go by and nothing really happens, and then all of a sudden, without any warning, something like this jumps out at you, knocking you out of your skin and turning you into someone you barely recognise.

Try as I might, I couldn't escape from the reality that was dawning on me. Whenever I tried to suppress the voices in my head chanting 'You're pregnant, you're pregnant,' and whenever I tried to deny it, another voice would pipe up elsewhere, taunting me to face it and accept the truth.

There were two personalities at loggerheads within me. One was screaming the truth at the top of her lungs; I didn't have much time for her. The other was my friend, the one who refused to admit it. Unfortunately, the first voice won, and in the end I had no choice but to confront the truth.

I'm pregnant.

My heart began to pound. I thought the fear would kill me.

I'm pregnant.

What did this mean? What would I do? How should

I act? Should I tell someone? Who? Janty? How would he react? One of my friends? Hayat? Leila? No, I couldn't tell them. They would push me away out of fear for their reputations. Mum? She'd be livid; she'd come down on me like a ton of bricks. My brother? Was I out of my mind? Should I just hand him a noose while I'm at it?

My fingers betrayed me and gravitated towards my belly. I could feel life growing inside me: an innocent child who was condemned before he had even seen the light of day. My hormones betrayed me and sided with my changing body. For the first time in my life, I was aware of a maternal instinct. An all-engulfing wave of love swept through me, and I was dominated by an irresistible desire to defend and protect this unborn child.

My child and I were one. He was me and I was him. We were two beings sharing one body. And yet we were rivals who could not live together in peace. His existence spelled a death sentence for me and I meant the same to him.

The options swarmed back and forth before my eyes. The common denominator between them all was death: his death. My child was condemned whichever way I looked at it. He could face termination alone, or be murdered with me, or be killed along with me and my brother or my father!

My imagination ran riot. What if... what if I chose the hardest option: to confront it head on? What if I chose not to carry out the death penalty myself? Who would carry it out instead? My dad? My brother? Or my cousin? Or could I keep them all out of it somehow and deal with the situation by myself? Should I tell Janty? Would he be able to protect me? If he decided to ask for my hand in marriage, my family would refuse outright. And it's impossible to imagine his family agreeing to such an insane idea. He's only twenty years old. He's a university student in the prime of his life. Getting married now could put a brake on his career and wreck his future.

I shut the door of my room and turned off the light. I wanted total darkness. I wanted to be alone. I wanted to die.

My eyes welled up with tears as I pictured my child as a valiant warrior battling to defend his right to life. He has me, his mother, to fight; and he has to fight my brother and my father. And then he has everyone else to contend with: our society and the whole world. I cried even more when, for a fleeting moment, I considered the possibility that Janty might let us down and cut us off, condemning my child to a life of shame, without a father or a real family to call his own.

I was filled with a sense of hatred for myself, and for everyone around me. I hated our culture and our religion, our traditions and our social prejudices. Where was the justice? Was it justice if I was condemned to death because I chose to preserve the life of my child?

Was I going to make a criminal of my brother—while he was still a teenager, while he was still at school? I was well aware of how our society operates. If my child and I were the first victims, then my brother would inevitably be next to fall. If I was the one who sullied my family's honour, then he carried the responsibility for reinstating that honour and washing away the shame.

I went over it all again and again, always coming back to the same question: what was my crime?

When I decided to fulfil my physical desires, it was only after I had accepted that my body belonged to me and no one else. I decided to grant my body its natural right and to exercise my rights as a woman, as a free human being who possessed the most basic thing any person can possess: a body. I believed that I had the right to use my body as I wished and that if I had sex it was no one's business but my own. It was a confidential matter between me and my partner. I knew full well that I could not change the world, and I hadn't had any reason to want to change it while I could trust in that confidentiality.

I considered myself an intelligent, educated woman. I knew my choices and the consequences of my actions. I did have some common sense: I knew how to take care of myself and how to protect myself. I learned how to use contraception so I could protect my body's right to privacy. I knew there was always a chance it wouldn't work, a very slim chance, but I decided to risk it. It was my right to take risks occasionally. Everyone takes risks, don't they?

But now, here I was facing one of the most difficult decisions of my life. Did I have it in me to tell the world where to go? To defend my right to live how I choose and be who I want to be? Or would I kill my baby and maintain my body's secret freedom?

My instincts tended towards telling the world where to go. But my fear held me back and pushed me towards sacrificing my child.

I almost did it. I almost executed my baby. But then I decided to involve Janty in the decision. We needed to share the responsibility—it takes two to tango, after all, and it was his baby, too.

***

I will never forget Janty's gutsy response when I told him about the baby. He proved what he had in him, the gallantry that flowed in his veins. He didn't hesitate for a moment before stepping into his new shoes as a father; he immediately took control of the situation, seizing the reins as protector of his family. When he hugged me tightly and rested his hand on my belly, I was struck by a feeling of security I had so badly missed over the last few days. That was when I knew that he was the man I wanted to spend the rest of my life with.

I was in pieces as I struggled to get the words out amidst a torrent of tears. I tried to tell him that I didn't want to mess up his future, that I was so scared and had no idea what to do. He waited until I had calmed down a little, and his words were composed and rational. We agreed to rule out the possibility of aborting the foetus. But we knew we couldn't go and tell my parents: the idea of getting married to legitimise the situation seemed out of the question. As far as my parents were concerned, marrying a man from another religion was a taboo; it was completely unthinkable. In fact, it was not much less of a disgrace than getting pregnant out of wedlock.

We decided that as a first step we would tell his mother,

as Janty was very close to her. Whatever they might think about him getting a girl pregnant outside of marriage, we thought they were unlikely to see it as a disgrace or an insult to their honour. They were more likely to recognise that their son was in trouble and needed their help.

In fact, as the man who stole my virginity and got me pregnant, Janty's life was under threat as much as mine. My family might decide to dispose of both of us to cleanse the shame and to send a clear message to other men to stay away from their daughters. So there was no time to lose: his mother had to think on her feet.

Once his father was in the picture, too, and they had assessed the scale of the catastrophe, they suggested we get out of the country and escape to his uncle in Sweden. We could try to resolve matters with my family and deëscalate the situation from there.

I kept quiet at home in front of my family for several weeks while we waited for the visas to come through. I spent most of the time in my room keeping out of sight, terrified someone might notice the changes in my body. I agonised over the thought of what a shock it would be for my mum and dad when they found out. Would they ever forgive me?

I was crying inside the day I bade everyone farewell, in silence. Not a single member of my family could read in my eyes what I was going through. I didn't dare kiss my dad on the cheek or give my mum a hug. All I took with me was my notebook for uni, a bag that I'd filled with a few essentials, some make-up, and my passport.

I set off for university like any other day, but this time

I didn't come back. I headed out into the unknown without any of my family having the slightest inkling. Society left me with no other choice. I was now in the hands of a wheel of fortune, an arrow spinning like a compass that would dictate the direction fate would take me. Fate had plucked me from roots that could no longer sustain me, and I was at its mercy as I set off with painful footsteps on the path ahead.

Janty and his parents met me outside the campus gate and they drove us to the airport. His mother hugged me and told Janty to look after me and the baby. His father took out a wad of cash and handed it to me, assuring me that he would take care of us while we were abroad, for as long as it took to resolve things. He had opened a bank account for Janty, and he promised to transfer enough money for both of us every month. He asked us to phone when we had arrived safely, and he said he would tell my family so they wouldn't exhaust themselves looking for me.

Sitting there on the plane, we sought comfort in silence. Janty held my hand, eager to reassure me that everything was going to be just fine, though I could see the worry on his face, too. I couldn't help thinking, with some sadness, about the countless women before me who must have found themselves in a situation like this. So many women must have paid the price with their lives and the lives of their children.

I felt so lucky at least to live in an era where we had the means to quickly transport ourselves away, out of sight, as if nothing had happened. As if I had died. Was it any different? Wasn't being forcibly removed from my life as I knew it tantamount to a kind of death?

***

Drifting off to sleep, I found myself in another world and another era. Everywhere was dust and crowds of people, so many that I couldn't make out individuals. I saw that I was kneeling in the sand. I looked down to see my hand cradling my stomach, soothing my baby, and rocking him so he didn't feel afraid.

I felt no fear as I peered at the faces of the crowd encircling me. My mind was hazy, not fully conscious, somehow detached from my body. I seemed to sit to the side, leaving my body to its fate, dispassionately watching the expressions flicker across the faces of the men, women, and children: anger, hatred, horror, and delight.

Every single one of them was armed with a stone. Stones of every shape and size. Sharp edges and corners impatient to tear my young body to shreds and attack my unborn child. Voices shouting and hurling curses, all mingling into one deafening hum so I could no longer make out what they were saying. But I could read it in their faces.

"Death to the whore!"

Pressing my hands against my chest, I bent my knees and dropped to the ground. In silence, I closed my eyes and waited. Seconds passed, each one feeling like an eternity, as the clamour of the crowd grew louder and louder.

"Death to the whore!"

Suddenly, a hush fell as a bearded man appeared, his face raging with anger. All eyes turned to him.

"He who is without sin may cast the first stone!" he bellowed at the crowd. "He who is without sin may cast his stone now!"

There was a moment of silence, followed by the sound of the stones falling. But not upon me; no, they were dropping to the ground. These stones fell, and the crowd's faces were laden with feelings of shame and disgrace.

The stones dropped to the ground that day, but it would not be long before that man would also fall, along with his words, and so would I. Wandering through the mists of time, I searched everywhere for that valiant man. I searched in vain for him or someone like him, or even someone with just a modicum of his strength, courage, and humanity.

Though I looked everywhere, I could find no men, only male beasts. The true men were maimed or killed off as masculinity fell prey to the clutch of violence. The male of the species had mutated into something that claimed authority over my body, my mind, and my soul. I escaped the stoning that day, but in another place and another time, I was burned at the stake. I escaped the stoning that day, but in another time, I was ravaged by a firing squad, I was hung, drawn, and quartered.

I huddled up in this hollow in the ground. Looking around again, this time I could see through the crowds, past them into the distance. I looked around me and saw not that I was not alone squatting in my shallow grave. Around me stretched hundreds of pits, thousands, millions, all the same.

And in each pit cowered a woman like me. Every single woman sat there in silence. Lost in the abyss, they could do nothing but submit their bodies to their executioners.

My tears fell. The tears of the women in the other pits also fell. Every tear struck against the motionless body of its owner as though trying to wash it. These tears didn't realise that no matter how they tried to cleanse a woman's body, it wouldn't change a thing. It would be better to strike the minds of men, stirring them to restore honour and grace to masculinity, and to restore femininity to life.

HAYAT

Everyone's life story must be equally insane

AMMAN usually seems huge—after all, it is a city of two million people, but then again, it often feels like a tiny village where everyone knows each other. Whenever two locals meet for the first time, it's no time at all before you realise how many friends or acquaintances you have in common.

My life has changed beyond recognition since I got the job as an air hostess. Of course, by its nature the work isn't easy, but it suits me perfectly. It takes me far from home for days at a time, and I've enjoyed a taste of the independence I was longing for. My relationship with Amr has been great, too; despite having to keep it secret, it has brought many moments of happiness and something of a sense of security.

Besides my affair with Amr, I have also developed a strong friendship with another air steward called Samir. Right from the start, I felt really comfortable and relaxed with him, as though he were a brother I didn't know I had. I'm not sure it was being in the air for hours at a time that detached us from the world around us, or if it's because we spent so many hours together at work, but we both opened up our hearts to one another in a very short space of time. He told me about his sexual orientation and his attraction to men, and I told him about my relationship with Amr.

Samir was the first gay person I'd ever met. I wasn't even really aware of what homosexuality was, beyond a few characters I'd seen in American films and TV shows. I was aware of the social prejudice and moral profiling surrounding gay people, which had a lot in common with the sort of rejection and stereotyping I always felt subject to, so I didn't have any prejudices when Samir entrusted me with his secret and shared with me part of his life that he shared with only a few select people.

Perhaps I feel safe with him because of the lack of sexual desire in his eyes when he looks at me—unlike every other man I seem to have come across in my life. Samir's absence of sexual feelings towards my gender doesn't mean he lacks a sense of responsibility towards me or a masculine instinct to want to protect me and defend me. It doesn't make him any less able to love me as a person and to cherish me as a close friend. And it certainly doesn't make him any less able to appreciate my appearance; he's always quick to compliment me on my hairstyle, a piece of jewellery I have on, or a new dress.

Whenever he speaks to his boyfriend on the phone, he speaks to him as though he were female, just in case anyone overhears the call. I've started to do the same thing: I address Amr using feminine verbs and pronouns, to avoid anyone finding out about us. Samir commented on it once. We laughed about it, a sad kind of laughter that betrayed the degree of unfairness in a society that forces our relationships to conform to one single format, making certain things permissible for men only, and only in one specific arrangement.

But I had a shock the other day when Samir told me his lover was getting married to fulfil the social requirements he felt were placed upon him. The more I heard about him, the more I couldn't believe the connection that my mind was starting to form. This character seemed very familiar. Suddenly, I realised that he was talking about my friend Leila and her fiancé, Ali.

Could it be possible that Leila's fiancé was Samir's lover? Was my mind playing tricks on me? Was I imagining this unbelievable connection between the different sides of my life? Why did life always insist on surprising me when it comes to sex, always revealing the deep rift between how things really are and how we portray them to society?

At first I wondered if I was I getting carried away with this story, and jumping to conclusions, when it could be just be a coincidence, and probably had nothing to do with my friend's situation. But the more I heard, the more I was convinced, and I found myself victim to a moral dilemma that left me feeling dizzy, confused, and guilty. Was there something in my character that made misfortune keep seeking me out?

It seemed it really was the same Ali… but why? Had he deluded himself into thinking he could protect Leila and that he'd found the answer he was looking for in life?

I found myself in an impossible position; how could I decide what to do? Here was Samir, who had trusted me with his secret just as I had told him things about myself that I would never tell anyone else. Samir had become my best friend, my closest confidant. He was as shocked as I was when I told him I was friends with Leila. He begged me not to utter a word.

And then there was Leila, who appeared to be the victim of this mad, foolish game Ali was playing, a cruel game which Samir and I unwittingly had become part of, and which burdened us with the responsibility of being silent spectators. Leila had distanced herself from me in the past few months since Ali came into her life, but she was still my friend; I loved her and I missed her. I missed getting together with the gang: Leila, Rana, and me.

Yes, I did have a lump in my throat when I thought about how she'd left us behind and abandoned our friendship just because she had found her life's companion. But that in no way justified me betraying her, and my silence on the matter would have an enormous impact on her future and could drop her into a life of lies for which she would pay the price when she realised the truth.

I knew the truth would seem like a stab in the back. She would certainly be shaken by it and probably very hurt. The dagger was in my hand like a medical scalpel. Would it be right for me to dress up as a doctor and offer my diagnosis, to expose to her the disease she was suffering from unwittingly? Was it right for me to hurt her in this way?

Is it a human right to know the truth, no matter how awful it is? Or isn't it our right to choose whether to hear the truth or not? But how can you choose, if life throws knowledge about things that concern you at the feet of other people, and puts the choice in their hands, giving them the power to chart the course of your future? Presumably we must bear responsibility for the choices we make on behalf of other people in our life, the choices we make about how to interact with them?

The whole world is insane when you think about it. Everyone's life story must be equally insane. We all fumble about in the dark trying to plan out the trajectory of our lives, although in truth it is determined by nothing more than our footsteps plodding on and on, our path twisting and turning with every little decision we make. Or perhaps it's the interaction of these decisions with our insane surroundings and the twisting trajectories of other people's lives that are no less insane than our own. Perhaps people's lives never stop intersecting and revealing a new truth with every minute that passes.

The crux of it was this: was it more morally justifiable to betray Samir and his secret or to betray Leila by failing to tell her the truth? Did the power of the truth swing the balance in Leila's favour? How could I even try to justify this morally when I myself had asked Samir to keep quiet about my affair with Amr? How would I feel if Samir told Amr's wife about us? If his wife and Samir were to become friends one day would it release him from the responsibility of keeping his promise to me? Would it make me feel better about betraying him if he did the same to me?

It was simpler and easier to choose to keep quiet, but instead I chose Leila. She didn't deserve to be cheated and misled in this way. Okay, I'm no saint, I don't have a halo, and I know I try to ignore other people's feelings when they clash with my needs and my desires, but I felt a duty towards Leila. I felt that I had a responsibility to protect her and to share the truth with her. So I picked up the phone and gave her a call just a week before the wedding.

"There's something really important you need to know about Ali," I said. "I can't tell you on the phone. I need to see you."

PART SIX

SALMA

Two weddings… two brides… two celebrations…

TWO *weddings… two brides… two celebrations…*
This phrase has been going round and round my
head, ever since I woke up early this morning to
hear my mother and Leila discussing the day ahead and the
final preparations for the wedding this evening. Today is
Leila's big day, and it's mine, too. Everyone has been getting
ready for Leila's wedding for months. But not mine—I've
been preparing for it by myself, silently, for just the last few
days.

Two weddings… two brides… two celebrations…

I've been muttering this to myself all week, and I was
still murmuring it as I parked up in front of the wedding
dress shop in Swéfiéh. Leila chose her dress two months
ago. Our mum and I came along to help her choose. She
was so excited, flitting between dresses like a Disney princess. I, on the other hand, felt suffocated at the sight of the
mountains of white fabric. I imagined the whole lot piled
up on the bodies of brides coming in at me from all direc-
tions. Every single bride stared at me with derision, cackling
sarcastic laughter that rang out across the store.

Two weddings… two brides… two celebrations…

I chanted to myself as I entered the store. This time I

was on my own. I tried to drive the image of the cackling brides out of my head. This time I was entering the shop as an *aroos*, a bride, just like them, and they had no right to laugh at me. But their faces wouldn't disappear from my mind; they were still there haunting me as I chose a dress. They all glared at me in silence. The laughter was gone from their faces, replaced by a look of sadness and pity.

"Do you have any black wedding dresses?" I asked the saleswoman. "I'm kidding," I added, seeing the alarm on her face.

I chose one of the loveliest dresses I could find as I wanted to look stunning on my wedding day. If the whole world was going to celebrate with me, then I had to be as beautiful as any other bride.

"*Two weddings... two brides... two celebrations...*" I hummed to myself as I carried the dress to the car and placed it in the boot.

***

And now, my big day has come. I watch in silent delight as everyone runs around doing everything they can to make Leila as pretty as a picture. No one pays the slightest bit of notice to my existence. No one realises it's my wedding day, too. I am the transparent bride, the invisible *aroos*. All alone, I look on in silence. I spin around with them in the fixed orbit around Leila.

The most important task for the day is to visit the make-up artist and hairstylist. I go with Leila and our mum, and our sister-in-law. It takes three hours to get our hair and make-up done to be ready for the evening. Leila takes the longest, of course, but Mum's make-up also takes forever as she keeps crying just as the stylist adds the finishing touches to her eyes, so then we have to wait for her to start all over again—several times.

Her tears are a mixture of joy for Leila and sadness about her leaving home, not realising that tonight sees the departure of not just one daughter, but two. You should always be careful what you wish for. All your wishes might come true one day, but not at all in the way you imagined.

Two weddings… two brides… two celebrations…

I drop my mum off at the wedding venue at the Hotel InterContinental, and tell her I'll be back shortly. I have it all mapped out. Everything I need is ready in the boot of my car. I set off towards Jabal al Hussein and from there to the Citadel. I want to look down from as high a vantage point as possible, so I can rain curses down on this oppressive city. The citadel district is the part of the city that carries its heritage and bears witness to its daughters' screams, to their pain. Today I want to confront my city, to scream in its face, and let my voice echo far and wide.

Yesterday I wrote a blog post in preparation for today:

There has existed a human custom since ancient times, across countless different cultures and civilisations, of sacrificing a person or persons in the event of a natural disaster, in the belief that the community was duty-bound to offer such a sacrifice to satisfy the angry gods or evil spirits. In many cases, the sacrificial victim was a woman, a virgin whom they presented as a symbol of fertility, in the hope of securing the gods' magnanimity.

The custom of human sacrifice is no longer practiced in modern societies due to the belief in these societies that violence can be avoided in the presence of a sound legal structure that imposes social justice. But when those laws fail to prevent injustice, it is difficult to avoid violence, and self-sacrifice becomes a credible solution.

Suicide bombings would not have become so widespread in the modern age were it not for this absence of political, social, and economic justice. The Palestinian woman who blew herself up in Tel Aviv, to cast a spotlight on the oppression of an entire people who did not benefit from legislation and international laws, is no different to the woman inside me who has had no support from modern social legislation in throwing off the legacies and the constraints that still restrict her relationships with others and her existence as a woman.

And so here I am today choosing to sacrifice myself, so that perhaps my image might be firmly impressed upon society's collective memory and in the hope of sparking a conversation that might result in social change, so that everyone, especially mothers, might relinquish some of the pressure they exert on their daughters and let them live the life that they picture for themselves.

***

I arrive at the Citadel and park my car on one of the side roads. I open the boot and take out everything I have ready for the night ahead: the wedding dress, my Yasmine doll, a picture of my nephew, my smartphone, and a razor blade.

As the sun sets amidst the Roman ruins, I slip through to the grounds behind the Citadel. I put down Yasmine and the other things while I hide behind a Roman column to change my clothes. It is just a few moments before I step out in full bridal regalia, a proud *aroos* standing at the head of the city, looking down from its summit, ready to sacrifice herself.

I place the photo of my nephew on the rock beside me and sit my doll, Yasmine, on the ground, her back to the rock. I prop my smartphone up on the rock opposite, and then I'm ready to start. I set up the camera to stream the video live to my blog, so the world can witness what I have to say. I position the camera to face me and press record. I pick up the razor blade. I raise my hand up to the sky and steel myself to deliver my speech.

"So you want me to be an *aroos*?" I holler at the top of my voice, addressing everyone in this city that I love so dearly.

"So you want me to be an *aroos*?" I shout even louder. Then a moment's silence, as I look directly at the camera.

"Here I am," I continue. "Your bride, my beloved city. Am I worthy of you, my love, my city? Am I good enough for you, Mum?"

The tears stream from my eyes and the blood bursts from my right wrist as I pass the blade across it. Blood splatters my face, and as I wipe my tears, I cover my face and my wedding dress with blood. I lift up my hand and I scream.

"This is the blood of your bride, Amman… the blood of your honour that you have saved up for a day like today."

I feel dizzy. I hear the echo of voices singing from afar, angelic voices singing as I enter the wedding hall on my special day.

"Salma, ya Salma. Our beautiful bride, our Salma… Salma, ya Salma. The virgin bride, our Salma…"

I almost lose my balance and tumble over, but I catch myself and I carry on.

"I've played by your rules and your customs. I've been obedient, chaste… I have never been with a man… I have excelled in my studies and in my work… I work hard to help my father pay the bills… I work hard to help my mother with the housework. But I have never been good enough."

"Salma, ya Salma. Our darling bride, our Salma."

"I deprived myself of what I desired and longed for in this world for your sake. But all that was not enough… it was never enough.

"Is this the blood that you were waiting to see on my wedding day?" I scream, as I slash the artery in my left wrist. "Is this the blood that proves I'm intact, that I'm pure and untouched in your eyes?"

I fall to the ground, unable to move. I look over at Yasmine. I crawl towards her. I want to hold her again before I leave this world. I sense voices approaching, growing louder and louder:

Salma, lovely Salma,
Our lovely bride, our Salma…
Our precious mother Salma…

Our darling sister Salma…

Salma's in her wedding dress,
See her weeping in distress.
Her silent sisters, painted fair;
Niqab or veil? Or flowing hair?
Subdued, suppressed, at work or rest,
They cower in fear when men are near.
Powder, lipstick; wax and pluck,
They wait with bated breath for luck
To bring at last
A man to shadow over them.

Salma spills her wedding blood,
The spinster's curse nipped in the bud.
Her silent sisters, chaste and fair,
Some veil their hair while some show theirs.
All wear their honour on their sleeves,
And cower in fear when men are near.
They cover up from head to toe,
Crush their dreams, search high and low
For anyone,
Any man to shadow over them.

Salma shows her groom disdain,
Shuts off her feelings, cuts her veins;
Her outraged sisters going spare,
So what if veiled or flowing hair?
They seize their rights, resist the stream,
Strong-willed, focused on their dream.
Armed with knowledge, toil away!
They know, for sure, that one fine day
They'll find the one:

A man who'll bring them light.

She falls down on her wedding night,
Stirs her sisters up, ignites
Them as she pulls her streaming hair;
Her scream, her blood: this isn't fair!
But let them fight for what is right,
For all our sisters:
May it bring them light.

Salma, lovely Salma,
Our lovely bride, our Salma…
Our precious mother Salma…
Our darling sister Salma…

"Go gently on, my sisters," I whisper. I close my eyes, muttering under my breath. "*Two weddings… two brides… two celebrations…*"

LEILA

How strange it is to see two sisters like this

HOW is it that fate can knock a person from the height of happiness to the depths of despair in the blink of an eye? How is it that one minute you're daydreaming, planning for the best night of your life, thinking you've found everything you wanted from life, that you've achieved everything you wanted to do, only to have fate cruelly snatch it all from your hands? Leaving you feeling lost, as though life has lost all flavour, afraid of even daring to think about happiness ever again.

Was it perhaps the curse of envy? Was it the evil eye of envy that made me a target for misfortune? Maybe the stars were aligned in such a way that my wedding was destined to descend into such a disaster. Or was it always written in my fate that I would never achieve full happiness, that tragedy would strike and rob me of the dearest, most precious person in my life?

I was in an odd mood when I woke up early on the day of my wedding, gloomy somehow, as though I could sense impending trouble. Was my heart trying to warn me against excessive happiness so as to lessen the impact as I fell? It was a strange feeling or, rather, a strange absence of feeling. I felt tense and anxious as I got the last things ready before the wedding, moving about like a robot, carrying out tasks without really being conscious of what I was doing.

Is it simple human nature? Do we crave something from afar, but when the time comes for us to achieve what we want, once it's there within reach, does our appreciation of it fade? Do we lose all ability to enjoy it? Or is it because we get so accustomed to dreaming about this goal that actually achieving it becomes tantamount to the death of the dream which has provided us with a sense of happiness and optimism all this time? Or is it an inability to believe that the dream is about to come true that prevents us from truly feeling it in a tangible way? Or is it perhaps that after achieving the object of our dreams, we uncover a kind of latent fear: the fear of losing something so precious, of destroying something so long awaited, and of plummeting back to square one?

I realise now that I wasn't looking out for Salma that day. In fact I barely spoke to her, and I didn't once ask her how she felt. I didn't understand when she hugged me close and whispered in my ear.

"Don't be angry with me," she said. "I love you so much."

I didn't give much thought at the time to her words and why she didn't want me to be angry. It didn't even occur to me to ask her what she meant. I thought perhaps I hadn't heard right and that it can't have been anything important. I was totally self-absorbed that day, convinced that it was all about me—it was my big day and I was the sun everyone revolved around. I didn't think about anyone else; it was up to them to pay attention to me and wait on me hand and foot.

Yes, I was extremely selfish. I failed to notice the sadness and pain in Salma's face. I was blinded by my desire for happiness, an egotistical impulse that kept my sister's feelings hidden from my sight. The whole time I've been engaged to Ali, I've stopped myself from thinking about the impact of my marriage on Salma. I assumed she was able to cope with it and that she wouldn't let it get to her. While she usually seemed upset when one of her friends or acquaintances got married, she hadn't shown any sign of that response to me getting married. On the contrary, she was always at my side, ready to support me and help me with everything that needed doing.

I feel this enormous guilt about it all. How could I cause so much pain to my sister, in cold blood, and yet without even noticing? The poor thing suffered in silence until it all came out in one huge explosion on my wedding day…

Oh, Salma, I miss you so much!

That day, at the wedding, we all got more and more anxious with every moment that passed by and still Salma was nowhere to be seen. At first, we tried not to worry and told ourselves that she would appear any minute now. When it had really been a long time since anyone had seen her, and she was refusing to answer her phone, my brother went out to look for her.

I was extremely tense by this point. I tried not to let the guests see I was upset, as I didn't want to spoil the party, but

I was asking about her constantly, while outwardly watching the dancing as if nothing was out of the ordinary.

We received the news the moment the band stopped for dinner. They all wanted to hide the news from me, but my mum fainted when she heard. In an instant, the wedding party descended into a funeral, and the joy collapsed into mourning.

Everyone left in shocked silence, until just Ali and I and our immediate families remained, and a few other relatives. Someone brought his laptop over and went online. He checked Salma's blog, and said that she had posted on it, and that she had killed herself. I didn't believe him at first. The rest of us didn't even know that Salma had a blog, and we couldn't fathom how she could be the blogger behind *The Jordanian Spinster*, one of the most popular blogs in Jordan.

The men in the family went off to find her, to find out if it was true. They tried to keep my father and my brother away from the horrendous scene, but they refused to be kept away. They couldn't believe it was true unless they saw it with their own eyes. I wanted to, too, but they wouldn't let me.

Salma was in a wedding dress just like mine. How strange to see two sisters like this, both brides on the same day. She was crying from behind the laptop screen, and I was crying in front of it. I couldn't believe what was happening before my eyes; I couldn't believe what my eyes were seeing. I wanted to tear my wedding dress to shreds. I wanted to rip it up, and rip up the wedding, the whole engagement, everything—to turn back time and be back at Salma's side.

To hug her and tell her that I'm not a bride, I'm not an *aroos*. To tell her that I don't want to be an *aroos*, I hate weddings and everything to do with them.

I cannot get her face and her voice out of my mind, and I don't think I ever will.

I wouldn't have been able to bear the pain of that day were it not for Ali. I had never even imagined the tenderness that I experienced as he held me in his arms that day. I was lost in floods of tears as he held me tight, kissing me on my forehead and wiping away my tears with his fingertips. Our first kisses, that I'd waited for so long, came when I had already lost all sensation and ability to enjoy them.

I refused to go home with him that night like any other bride. I didn't feel able to move forward with our new life. I wanted to cling on to my old life still, the life that I knew with Salma.

So I went back to our room—mine and Salma's. I imagined her with me just as it's always been. I closed my eyes and sensed her presence in the bed beside mine. I could smell the cigarettes that she smoked by the window every night. I opened my eyes and was just about to ask her to stop it, but she wasn't there.

I fumbled around in her things and found a packet of cigarettes and a lighter. I pulled out a cigarette and lit it. Standing where Salma usually stood by the window, I smoked as she did, as if it were an apology to her, a way of telling her that I'm here with her, at her side, that I'm all hers.

I was trapped in this mood for a week. I kept on

refusing to leave, and the only thing that could persuade me to go back to my husband's place was my father and mother insisting. Even though our family had experienced a tragedy, the likes of which none of us had ever been through, and these were exceptional circumstances, nevertheless custom dictated that a bride cannot stay anywhere other than her husband's house for this long after the night of the wedding.

Ali came to visit us every evening. He was very patient and understanding. He didn't seem annoyed by the situation, and didn't push me to do anything. He let me go at my own pace, while it was my mother and father who started putting pressure on me, insisting that this couldn't continue and that I should go home with him. I felt drained as I finally set foot in our flat. I was engulfed by a feeling of guilt towards Salma that made me unable to be the bride that I was supposed to be.

Ali and I agreed to wait forty days before consummating our marriage out of respect for Salma. When the fortieth night came I didn't know what to do. Ali didn't take the initiative and ask for his marital right. Maybe it was out of respect for my feelings and he was waiting for me to be ready. But I was too shy and embarrassed to say anything or to reveal my desire for sex, even though it was to someone I loved and who was my legitimate husband.

That night, memories of events surrounding the wedding came back to me. Two weeks before the wedding, I heard the news about Rana getting pregnant and eloping with Janty to Sweden. I could hardly believe my ears. I couldn't believe that Rana was capable of such a thing. How could she sneak out of her family's house in secret and bring all that shame and disrepute on herself? My reaction was partly to worry about how it would affect me personally, what it would mean for my reputation. We were really good friends at university, so our reputations were inextricably linked. Would I be tarred with the same brush?

I decided not to tell Ali. I didn't want him or his family to hear. A few days later, I went to see Hayat to find out what she wanted to tell me about Ali, because judging by her voice on the phone it was something alarming, and I kept imagining all kinds of catastrophes. But perhaps the real catastrophe was giving her a chance to speak. I never ever imagined such audacity, such an insult as to come to me a week before my wedding day to tell me that my fiancé was gay.

Gay? What? Was Hayat out of her mind?

"Ali's gay." That was what she said. I couldn't comprehend what that even meant. How could he be gay when there he was, my fiancé, everything I could hope for from a man? But she even had the nerve to suggest that to be gay didn't necessarily mean being effeminate. And then she had the cheek to ask if he had kissed me before or touched me intimately while we were engaged.

I screamed at her to shut up. Ali had always been the perfect gentleman. That fact that he hadn't molested me sexually during our engagement was because he respects me as an Arab woman with an innate sense of morality and religion, not because he's gay. Even if he had been gay in the past, even if he had had sex with men in the past, as she was suggesting, then that must have been because he didn't have a woman in his life to fulfil his needs.

The past is the past. Now, Ali loves me and he's marrying me, and he isn't gay any longer. She should have just kept her mouth shut rather than starting to spread vicious, hurtful lies like that.

I told her I no longer considered her a friend and she was not welcome at my wedding. So that's another reason why my wedding was so lacking in joy. I had been so looking forward to that evening and to sharing the celebrations with Rana, Hayat, and Salma. But in fact none of them was there. And without my friends, there was no happiness, just a gaping hole and a sour taste.

But that was weeks ago. Now I was ready to put it all behind me and move forward. I was more than a little afraid of my first sexual encounter, as I had never been with a man before. The few snippets of advice and information I had gleaned from my mum and my friends were not enough to put my mind at ease. The most important advice I had, I think, was to leave it to him to be in charge, as men liked to take the lead in a sexual relationship, or at least for it to seem that way to them. If I showed too much desire or took the initiative, I risked giving him the impression that I was sexually experienced, that I'd already been with another man before getting married. But the contradictory advice I had seemed so confusing and only made me feel more nervous about it all.

Ali read my willingness in my gestures and in the way I dressed and did my make-up. I straightened my hair and put on perfume, making myself ready for him. He came over to me and kissed me on my forehead. Hugging me, he stroked his hand across my cheek and ran his fingers through my hair.

His head moved towards mine and our lips drew closer until they touched. He was gentle as he moved closer, as if he sensed my nervousness and my fear. And I could also sense the same feelings in him.

I felt for a moment that this was something we had to do, something that had to happen, for us to lay the foundation for our marital life together.

I felt a shiver of excitement when his tongue touched mine. I let my hand reach up to his head to pull him close. He pulled away a little and looked into my eyes, then took off his shirt and began to unbutton mine, his fingers trembling. I felt even more scared, and more excited, too, when he took off the rest of his clothes and took me in his arms.

The night didn't go smoothly. It wasn't easy. Ali was as nervous and embarrassed as I was, so there was nothing I could do but put aside some of my awkwardness to help him. He seemed shy to touch my breasts, so I gently encouraged his hands to pass that way. He also needed time before he was ready to come inside me, and I also kept asking him to stop or to slow down when he was just about to.

It was hard, it was painful, but in the end we managed it, and our marriage was consummated.

ALI

It was all very attractive, but it didn't turn me on

A man can survive a test with honour or he can drown in disgrace. When I was a child, I used to deal with my fear of exams by not letting myself think about the consequences. I would work hard, cramming what I could, and then place my trust in God, as I entered the exam room feeling strong. I would scribble down whatever I had managed to memorise and hand the paper over to the teacher as quickly as I could.

My wedding night was the scariest exam I ever had to face. The dread seeped into every part of me, but like any other exam, I approached it with my trust in God. My mental preparation consisted of consulting a few of my gay friends, some who were married and some who weren't, asking them for tips on how to survive the process where so much was at stake. I had never tried having sex with a woman before and I had never been in the slightest bit attracted by a woman's body. Not even Leila. As much as I love her, in one sense—she just doesn't turn me on.

Some of my friends couldn't offer any advice because they couldn't imagine putting themselves in such an 'awful' situation as this. Some of them suggested I take Viagra to get warmed up. And someone suggested booking a room for Samir in the hotel, next to the bridal suite, and starting the night off with Samir to get me in the mood, before culminating things with Leila. Of course, this was totally impractical and was rejected straight out by both me and Samir. But I also found it difficult to imagine myself in this situation, and therefore preferred to just wait and see what happened, just as I used to at school.

But then, the exam was postponed, and the period of dread and fear leading up to the wedding night spilled over and dragged on another forty nights. They say fortune and misfortune are two sides of the same coin. I'm ashamed the thought even occurred to me, although it did seem apt. I felt a great sadness at the loss of Salma and at the pain and grief that hit Leila, but deep down there was a part of me that breathed a sigh of relief that we could postpone the dreaded moment. It was a welcome pretext to cover up my struggle for another forty nights. It seemed likely we would put it off when, on the day of the wedding, we heard the terrible news that Salma had committed suicide, and then we made it definite a week later, when Leila joined me at our place. I felt an enormous pang of guilt, when my suggestion that we postpone our first night together was taken as mark of respect for Salma. But when day forty approached, I couldn't put it off any longer. I simply had to man up and take the plunge. It is excruciatingly difficult to force yourself to do something that your body and soul wholeheartedly rejects. And it's even harder when it's something you cannot escape.

There was no escaping Leila. From the way she dressed it was clear that she was ready and was expecting me to take the initiative. She had straightened her hair and put it up in a seductive way. She had put eyeliner and lipstick on, and a nice fragrance wafted from her. It was all very attractive, but it didn't turn me on.

I moved closer to her. I put my arm around her and kissed her on the forehead and then on the lips. Her fragile, delicate body and her feminine perfume quashed all desire in me. For a moment I panicked, but I managed to calm myself down. I was afraid she would read something in my body language. And even more afraid that my body wouldn't play along and I'd find myself in a very awkward position.

I closed my eyes and tried to summon up the desire. I closed my eyes and imagined it was Samir in my arms instead of Leila. I was betraying her from the very first night our bodies came together. I couldn't complete the task without a man being present, in my mind's eye, and without the help of Viagra.

It certainly wasn't easy. Without lust or desire, it wasn't sex; it was a feeling of repulsion, not of attraction. I had to endure it, to grin and bear it, though my whole body screamed at me to run. I tried to go with the flow and to move with her like when I'm making love to Samir. So I kissed her now and again and when my tongue touched hers I could sense her excitement, but I just felt queasy, this feeling of repulsion. I pulled away a little. Then I braced myself, took her in my arms, and kept going.

I did complete the task that night. But it was a victory devoid of pleasure. I don't know how Leila felt about it, if she sensed that something wasn't right, that there was something that would haunt us throughout our married life. Perhaps her lack of experience would mean she didn't have high expectations when it came to sex. Hopefully she might have convinced herself that you can't judge things by the first night, and that our nerves would settle with time.

But not me: I'm even more afraid now of the days ahead and the times to come. As newlyweds, we will have to have a lot of sex. The first time was unbearably difficult, but I'm fairly confident it's not going to be any easier next time, or the time after that…

PART SEVEN

RANA

She and I are alike in so many ways

STOCKHOLM must be one of the most beautiful capitals in the world. The city is made up of fourteen islands linked by fifty-seven bridges. The architecture is stunning. The buildings stand squeezed side by side, in a dazzling array of colours, with pastels, reds, and yellows very prominent, quite unlike far-off Amman where everything is painted white. Everywhere are large expanses of green and so much water that I felt like I'd arrived in another world, unimaginably far from what I was used to seeing from the window of my room in Amman.

But all this beauty doesn't mean much to me. I'm not a tourist here, I'm a refugee. I'm on the run with my boyfriend, though we're still just students. I'm a fugitive, carrying inside me an innocent child who will open his eyes to see a country very far from his own, and to see a mother an exile from her family who are thirsty for her blood.

My dad hit the roof when Janty's father told him on the phone. He launched into a barrage of furious threats and curses, and Janty's father's assurances that they would make good the situation, and that Janty would marry me in a Christian ceremony in a Catholic church in Sweden, did nothing to calm him down. The photos Janty and I sent him of our wedding ceremony, the *iklil*, didn't help much either.

We organised the wedding in a hurry just days after arriving in Stockholm. We had a lot of help from Janty's uncle who had emigrated to Sweden with his family. Initially he opposed the idea of Janty marrying me in a church, on religious grounds, but he then bowed to the circumstances, accepting that it was a charade we simply had to play along with.

Our wedding pictures are rather sad and lifeless. They don't show crowds of family and friends crammed into the church hall as in normal family weddings in Amman. My family has disappeared from around me. I've had to say goodbye to my childhood dream of seeing them all around me on my wedding day to celebrate the joyful occasion with me. Instead, the pictures show an orphan. In some I'm there in a white dress standing next to Janty in a black suit. In others, the two of us are surrounded by Janty's uncle's family. Janty's uncle is on his right, his aunt, in a headscarf, is on my left, and their two sons are on the end next to their mother.

The men of the family in Amman got together and took a collective decision to disown me. They forced my parents to agree to cut off relations with me because, in their opinion, I had sullied the family's reputation and tarnished it with disgrace.

According to Jordanian society, my pregnancy is felt to have stripped not only my honour, but also that of my entire immediate and extended family. From now on, my shame will haunt my female cousins, too, and no suitors will come anywhere near them, unless my parents wash their hands of me and the whole family cuts me off.

Generally, the principle is that only killing me can wash away the shame, but thanks to the distance, and the fact that not all the men in the family are completely insane, they decided that in this case disowning me was sufficient.

What hurts most about it all is the position I've put my father in. I've always been so close to him, ever since I was a little girl. I can't bear to see sadness in his eyes, and it's painful to imagine him bowing his head in shame in front of the other men of the family.

I keep remembering the day my cousin came and threatened me at uni. I can imagine him now sitting there smugly with the other men, brimming with pride about how manly he looks, at the expense of my father.

One of the hardest things to deal with is my father cutting me off and refusing to talk to me on the phone. My mother has also been angry with me, but when I disappeared, she seemed to be on the verge of a breakdown more from worrying about me than from anger. So she hasn't cut me off, at least; she calls me every day in secret to check that I'm okay. She whispers to me how much she loves me, and floods the handset with tears. What bothers her the most is losing me, and my being so far away, and she doesn't care in the slightest that my family blames her for bringing me up badly, saying it was her fault I ran away.

The area that Janty and I have moved to is called Radmansgatan. It's a quiet neighbourhood very close to the modern city centre as well as to the old town, Gamla Stan.

It's easy to get around Stockholm as there's a metro linking all the districts together and nowhere is more than a few minutes away. It has been tough getting used to the cold weather, as we arrived in late October when it was already as cold as the harshest time of year in Amman, in January. I couldn't believe that even colder weather was in store. I couldn't help feeling worried about it and depressed by the short days with the sun setting so early.

But the Swedes' warmth and friendliness, and Janty's loving hugs, make up for the cold of winter and the lack of sunshine. In a matter of days a strong friendship developed between me and Charlotta, our Swedish neighbour. Charlotta is Snow White in every way: her immaculate beauty and her pure heart. Her face is so bright it glows, and her heart seems to radiate compassion and love. She has two angelic little girls: the eldest is four and the second is only a few months old.

Charlotta had tears in her eyes and her cheeks burned red when I told her our story, about how Janty and I had to escape to Sweden. She and I are alike in so many ways, having been through such similar experiences, but in a different place and a different culture. She got pregnant by her boyfriend at the same age as me and moved in with him. For her it was a personal decision which certainly wasn't something that put her life at risk. Now they are both living together under one roof raising their two gorgeous children without needing to be married by a priest or a sheikh or needing an official piece of paper from the state sanctioning their relationship.

They are planning to get married next summer, although not because they need to. Their relationship, which would be seen as illegitimate in our country, has not caused them the slightest difficulty or trouble over the years; neither is it a source of shame or a reason for them to be ostracised by society. Far from it; they enjoy the same full set of rights as anyone else. As Swedish citizens, they are eligible to take two full years' parental leave: one year for the mother and one for the father. Charlotta decided to stay at home to look after her new baby girl for the first year, but she'll be returning to work in a few months, while her boyfriend Johnny will look after her for the second year.

All this is a source of amazement to me and I can't help feeling envious. Swedish society is so civilised that something that is a social catastrophe back home has evolved into something so ordinary that no one bats an eyelid. All I can do is compare it to our situation in Jordan. It saddens me that with all the economic difficulties my people face, we add further complications to our lives with all our oppressive social restrictions.

For an unmarried mother raising two young girls, Charlotta seems incredibly happy and relaxed to me. She doesn't have to worry about their monthly income or social expectations that would place further burden on her shoulders. She doesn't have her own car or an expensive flat in an upscale district to pay for. She lives in a rented house, small and unassuming. Two bedrooms: one for her and Johnny, and another for the two girls. But her life is simple. She has everything she needs and she is not dragged down by financial need or social imperatives.

She is very quiet and usually smiling. Anger is an expression I've rarely seen on her face, only when confronted by a case of injustice. It's happened twice since I've known her. The first time was when I told her my story, and the second was when she read the news about the latest assault on Gaza. She cannot stand by passively in the face of injustice; she abhors it. On the eve of the war, for example, she wrapped her children up in a mountain of clothes and went out with her boyfriend to join the swarms of protestors on the streets of Stockholm condemning the Israeli aggression. The day she heard my story, it was all she could do to hold herself back from grabbing the handset when I was on the phone to my mum and screaming at my family to respect me and respect my wishes. She has done so much to help me. She provided me with the addresses of all the Swedish social institutions that deal with immigrants, and she has always been by my side and ready to give me the best advice about life in Sweden.

We went out one day for *fika*—coffee and cake Swedish style—at a café in the city. As usual, Charlotta translated the headlines in the daily newspaper into English for me. One of them was talking about the spread of hymen-reconstruction operations across Sweden, something I was stunned to hear about. I would expect it in an Arab newspaper, given how sacred we still hold virginity. But I never thought I would read about it in a Swedish newspaper, in a country so proud of its openness and sexual freedom. But Charlotta quickly filled me in on the background and explained that these operations were becoming widespread among the Arab and Muslim minorities in Sweden, where Muslims now constitute about five percent of the Swedish people. Integration is posing a serious challenge to the state and to society as a whole.

I was astonished to realise the power our cultural heritage exerts over us. It knows no geographical or social boundaries. It is a form of baggage we carry with us wherever we go, and it seems that small immigrant communities grow up looking just like the parent community they moved away from. The problems faced by Arabs in Sweden these days are not much different to the problems back home.

Arab women carry the weight of the past with them wherever they go, and for Arab men, their sense of honour remains steadfastly linked to what's to be found between the thighs of their womenfolk, no matter whether they're in Amman or Cairo, Chicago or Stockholm.

I can't help wondering, do we Arab women have any chance of changing this reality and updating our society with a new set of assumptions? Or is the only way out restricted to those lucky few who manage to break the ties to their former Arab society and throw themselves wholeheartedly into the arms of their adopted homes?

LEILA

What if Hayat had been right when she told me about Ali?

I know I'm not alone in finding it hard sometimes to make sense of the expectations Jordanian society places on us. There is a set of minimum achievements we're all supposed to accomplish, and if you fail to tick all the boxes, you are seen as a disappointment and this eats away at the respect people show you. The first hurdle is to go to university and get a degree, although more importance is attached to getting married, and in the uncontested third place is the requirement to procreate.

But that is not all. Your success at university is judged by the class of degree you're awarded, and a marriage is judged by the age of the bride and by the groom's income. And so, too, with having babies. Though things are more relaxed nowadays, your success on becoming a parent is still judged on the sex of the baby. Top marks for a boy—distinction!—and just a regular pass for a girl. If the firstborn is a daughter, the parents will keep trying until they have a boy. If a boy comes first, well, then the pressure is on to produce a brother for him!

Thank God, I was spared the nagging from my family and the constant questioning from my mother-in-law about when I was going to produce a child. It was less than three months into our marriage before I realised I was pregnant. Ali and I decided to keep things simple and not attempt to plan things; we wouldn't use contraceptives, but neither would we put ourselves under pressure.

Everyone was delighted when they heard that I was pregnant. Ali and I hoped for a boy to join our small family, my father wanted another grandson to join his growing clan, and Ali's mother was also eager to rejoice over her first grandson. So I knew God was gracious when we found out from the scan that it was indeed a boy. Although deep down I longed for a baby girl I could call Salma in honour of my sister, I admit I enjoyed the admiring looks when people heard I was having a boy; I equally enjoyed the increase in interest shown to me by Ali, his mother, and my family. I saw a sparkle of delight in my mother-in-law's eyes, and all of a sudden she was gushing with pride and praising me constantly in front of her family and friends.

Overnight her way of addressing me changed from Leila to Oum Hassan, assuming my unborn child would take the name of her deceased husband. While I had expected my child to be given that name, out of respect for Ali and in accordance with tradition, I was still hoping for a brief discussion about it between my husband and me, or at least to be asked my opinion, not just to have the decision imposed on me by my mother-in-law.

The early days of pregnancy were hard. I woke up exhausted in the morning and sometimes I felt sick, too. To make things matters worse, I also had a serious bout of the flu that kept me in bed for over a week. My appetite became very bizarre. I started to crave food I'd never really liked before—and I was ravenous. The herb mix *zatar* became my constant companion at every meal and in between meals. Sometimes I'd sneakily dip my finger into the bowl and lick it, but when that wasn't enough I'd fill whole desert spoons, devouring it straight from the bowl like soup.

But the weirdest thing, and the thing that bothered me the most, was the feeling of aversion towards Ali that came over me in the first months of pregnancy. I couldn't bear him being anywhere near me. I got flustered and my heart would race, as I felt a wave of negative emotions wash over me. I don't know why I felt like this, but I suppose it was probably just to do with being so tired. Maybe it was hormonal—another physical symptom like the cravings? Or perhaps it was linked on a subconscious level to how worried I was about our sex life and in particular about Hayat's words which were still haunting me.

Ali never seemed to show any sign of sexual desire towards me. Although he was always very sweet and affectionate, and he inundated me with the kisses on the cheek or on my hand and always gave me a hug whenever the opportunity presented itself, he definitely showed less and less interest in having sex. If he did ask for it, he'd approach it gingerly as if it were a chore rather than something he wanted to do. When I got pregnant, he stopped asking for sex altogether, as if he had found an ally in my pregnancy that relieved him of the duty.

These whispers of doubt were a real blow to my

self-confidence. I became very depressed and struggled with my sense of femininity. Once I was a few months pregnant, that feeling of aversion towards Ali disappeared and was replaced by the opposite: sexual desire and a longing for affection and intimacy with my husband. At the time I staved off these thoughts and reassured myself that it was probably normal for him to keep his distance from me when my body was undergoing so much change; after all, my growing belly and swollen arms and legs were probably far from attractive.

But this distance between us continued after Hassan was born, and things were no better in the months that followed. He carried on seeming cold towards me, and the obligatory sex we did have became less and less frequent as time went by.

I didn't know what to do, who to turn to. I would have spoken to Salma if she were still alive; she was my closest friend and she understood me best. Perhaps I could have turned to Rana if I hadn't broken off my friendship with her when she got pregnant and ran off with Janty. And under different circumstances, if it hadn't been for what had happened between Hayat and me, then she might also have been an ideal person to talk to about it. She always used to give the best advice when it came to the opposite sex. She had an opinion about everything and always seemed so worldly-wise. But now things were different and I no longer considered her a friend. In fact, just thinking about her made my heart race and my blood boil.

I struggled to suppress the awful thoughts that kept

floating to the surface of my mind. What if Hayat had been right when she told me about Ali? Or did she simply plant a seed of doubt in me and create a problem where there might never have been one? Perhaps my paranoia was affecting how I behaved towards Ali and that was putting him off? Was I exaggerating something that was probably normal for newlyweds? I couldn't help wondering whether our sex life was something that bothered Ali, too. But maybe it didn't even cross his mind. Was he satisfied with our sex life? I was too shy to ask him about it.

The only person I had to ask about it was my mum. As shy as I was to ask her advice about sex, I desperately needed her support. I didn't mention what Hayat said about Ali being gay. I raised the topic in a calm and gentle way because I didn't want to freak her out, and I told her a little bit about our sex life and how worried I was that he was avoiding me. She quickly dismissed my concerns, saying I was making a mountain out of a molehill. As far as she was concerned, frigidity between couples was something inevitable and, sadly, the daily grind of married life was often enough to suppress the desire.

She told me for the first time about the problems my father had with his libido. They hadn't had sex for over twenty years. She acknowledged that it was perhaps unusual for the fire to burn out so quickly for a newlywed couple, but insisted that it wasn't anything to worry about, and that I had enough on my plate with looking after my baby, the house, and my husband, without getting distracted by these harmful ideas.

Try as I might, though, I just couldn't get these destructive thoughts out of my head. They darkened my mood, making me depressed about my role as mother and housewife. I felt ugly and frumpy, and like I had nothing feminine left about me. I had let myself go when I was pregnant and it wasn't any easier after Hassan was born.

But I had become a mother to a beautiful boy, my little darling who looked just like his father. He had no trouble getting a smile out of me: he only had to blink his eyes or a pout his little lips, and he wiped away my frown. It turned out Hassan really was plenty to keep my hands full and distract me from my dark thoughts and my misgivings. He give me a new compass and a new direction to my life, which had become, just as I suppose it is for most mothers, linked to the happiness of my son, and to his life and his future.

I couldn't fault Ali when it came to his duties as a father. He was always there at Hassan's beck and call. He would rush to him when he cried and would help me with feeding him and at bath time. He never grumbled or complained about being tired, even when he was robbed of sleep for hours at a time, when Hassan screamed and cried throughout the night. He was full of tenderness towards Hassan and me, and he did whatever he could to look after us, and make us comfortable and happy. Perhaps all this was him trying to compensate for what he couldn't give me in the bedroom, because he spoilt me rotten and showered me with gifts. The latest was the car of my dreams, a Porsche Cayenne, which he surprised me with when Hassan was born.

Unfortunately, this loving, kind way he treated me eventually just made me feel more confused than ever and started to drive me crazy. I couldn't claim he was a bad husband, although I found myself inventing problems and looking for the tiniest flaws that I would blow up out of all proportion. The fact is I had a need within me and I longed for a man to satisfy it whom I knew was all mine. I would push it away, but then this urgent feeling would flare up in moments of anger that I would regret later.

I found myself turning to God and to prayer. It finally seemed to be the right moment to make the decision I had always put off. I surprised Ali one day by telling him that I felt I'd grown closer to God and that I was ready to wear the veil. He didn't object; instead he was happy about it and was very supportive of me. He encouraged me to see it as something to celebrate and took me out that night for dinner at our favourite Italian restaurant in Jabal Amman.

***

All of this internal conflict came to a climax one evening when all my fears turned out to be well founded, no matter how much I wanted to deny them. I couldn't believe it when the truth came up and grabbed me by the neck.

It was a few days after his first birthday when Hassan took his first steps. I was overjoyed. They were cautious steps at first, but every shuffle translated into a symphony in my head. Hassan was pleased with himself, too, delighted with his newfound mobility and ability to explore his surroundings. When Ali popped out to the bathroom, Hassan seized on the chance to explore his dad's study. I rushed after him, afraid that he might break something or hurt himself. Hassan spotted his father's laptop and quickly headed for it. I hurried to catch him and move the laptop before he could get his hands on it. But as I went to pick it up and get it out of his reach, I was startled by what I saw on the screen.

There was a chat application open, and another window had a list of strange names with pictures of naked men beside each one. Some of them were of a face or a bare chest, but some showed a naked butt or a penis. At the bottom of the screen was a flashing alert saying there was an unread message from the 'Knight of Amman.' I clicked on it and was horrified by the animated icons that popped up of men kissing each other and having sex in various disgusting positions. My eyes quickly scanned over the conversation, this shocking sexual dialogue between an 'Iraqi in Amman,' presumably Ali, and this other man.

My head was spinning and my arms were too weak to hold Hassan. I let him squirm away and slip to the ground, and then I fainted to the ground myself. I don't know how long I was out.

HAYAT

*I have never really fit into the restrictive mould of what
is considered a healthy relationship*

SOMETIMES I'm amazed by my ability to turn over
the page to end one intimate relationship and start
another in no time at all. Well, that's what happened
to my relationship with Amr. Despite the wonderful
moments we spent together, I decided that the time had
come to move on and to end things quickly—no hesitation,
no looking back. All I needed was a morning with a clear
head to work things out in my mind. It was as if a lamp
suddenly came on and lit up everything around me.

Love is strange. It makes you simmer away for months,
sometimes years. It makes you build your entire life around
the one you love. You set up your world and paint everything around you with his spirit, his smell, his touch. But,
as abruptly as love arrives, so it departs—just like that. It's
as if you push a button to switch on the bright glow of new
love and then press it again to switch the light off, and you
go back and redecorate your world without the colours of
your beloved.

Why does my happiness always seem to rest on someone
else's unhappiness? Why do I always leave myself at the

mercy of unhealthy relationships that lead to nothing but pain and grief?

My mind was swarming with questions like these, and it all led me towards a split-second decision that I felt I had to act on spontaneously. It was one of the most important decisions of my life, and it gave me a sense of freedom and an unprecedented ability to seize the reins to my life and steer myself in a direction of my own choosing.

Although I missed Amr terribly for a few days, I was quick to replace my feelings for him with newfound feelings that sprang up for another man. It was a chance meeting somewhere over the Atlantic Ocean, in the aisle of an aircraft travelling from New York to Amman, with a man from distant shores.

Our eyes met for a moment as I handed him his meal and he handed me his heart, as he told me later on. In fact, he claimed that I stole his heart without any kind of introduction or prior warning the moment I softly spoke those fateful words, "Chicken or beef, sir?"

John is very different from all the men I've ever known in my life and who have ever occupied a place in my heart. He has ruddy cheeks, blue eyes, and not a hair on his head, and his face is creased with wrinkles, testifying to his forty years of age. He was on his way to Amman as a senior economic adviser on a USAID project in Jordan.

Whether or not I was a virgin was irrelevant to him, and he didn't judge me on my past relationships when I started to open up to him and we started getting close. He believes in sexual freedom and in a person's right to have multiple sexual relationships, even after marriage. He told me he was convinced that our human nature tends towards polygamy and that committing to one single sexual partner goes against our natural disposition and instincts as human beings. At first I found this idea very alien, because my concept of marriage was built on a commitment between two people and on sexual fidelity to each other. What was the benefit of marriage if there was no sexual fidelity?

But he sees it differently. He feels that marriage is a contract between two people who exchange love for one another and seek to make each other happy, to satisfy their various desires, and to help each other through life's ups and downs. If one person in the couple has special wishes or desires, then true love is granting your partner the freedom to achieve this, even if it involves someone else, and it shouldn't affect your freedom to fulfil your own needs and desires.

I wondered how jealousy fit into it all. I didn't think I would be able accept the idea that my husband was making love to another woman. And wouldn't he be jealous of me if I did the same? But as far as John is concerned, jealousy and love are so closely linked that we might believe at first glance that it is a healthy response, whereas in fact it is based on weakness and a lack of self-confidence; it is a sign that a relationship lacks strength. If he were to feel jealous of me enjoying time with another man, whether it was a sexual encounter or not, that would be pure egotism, arising from his weak character and a selfish desire to dictate to me how I spent my time. That's not true love. Love must be free of egotism, he argues; it must rise above jealousy, and not be tarnished by the concept of ownership.

He admits that there is no escape from jealousy, that it is intrinsic to our human nature, but he sees it as an internal feeling that an individual should try to resolve within himself or learn to live with. It does not give him the excuse to impose his control over the person he loves or to create restrictions on her freedom that reduce her chance of happiness.

What about the risk of falling in love with someone else with whom we may find more sexual pleasure than we found with our chosen life partner? John believes that the risk of falling in love with someone else is a normal risk that accompanies any relationship between two people. It isn't just about having sex. Love is more than sex. If something happens that threatens the marital relationship, it is the duty of both parties to deal with it internally, to overcome those feelings and fulfil their solemn vows to one another, and to uphold the sanctity of marriage. But if the love between a couple fades, and love appears in either of the partner's lives for someone else that is stronger, then separation is the ideal option. No one wants to live in a relationship that makes them feel miserable.

These seemed to me to be strange principles for a relationship, as they were ideas I'd never come across before, but I didn't feel uneasy talking about it as I'm certainly used to unusual relationships in my life. I guess I have never really fit into the restrictive mould of what is considered a healthy relationship in our society. It wasn't long before I felt quite at home with these ideas. They seemed to suit me and my life quite well. A certain amount of freedom increases the strength of a relationship, after all, and helps consolidate the degree of respect each partner has for the other and for our choices in life.

Although I really liked John, and his way of thinking made an impression on me, and although the age difference between us would normally suggest an unequal relationship where the stronger party (he) would tend to dominate over the weaker party (me), in fact, for the first time in my life, I felt a sense of autonomy. My relationship with him didn't rob me of my free will or my ability to make decisions for myself, as had been the case in my past relationships; but rather it gave me the strength that I had been looking for all this time and the feeling that there was someone standing behind me, supporting me as a whole person who is in charge of her own life and who possesses the keys to unlock her desires.

We had only been seeing each other a few months when he asked me to marry him. We had talked before, indirectly, about how his contract would end in a few months and he'd have to go back to the US, and this would all come to an end. But he would always correct me when I said that, insisting he would take me with him. I'd just laugh; I never took it seriously.

But I was amazed when he pulled out all the stops and set up the perfect scene to propose to me, just like in the movies. He took me out for a lovely romantic dinner to celebrate our six-month anniversary. He told me how intensely he loved me and how much he adored being with me. He said he'd found the girl he'd been looking for, that he'd been searching all the time in the wrong country. He said there was something about me, something about my character that enchanted him, and that he hoped we'd be able to spend the rest of our lives together. Since he couldn't stay here to be with me, he was hoping I would agree to move to be with him.

Suddenly, he pulled out of his jacket pocket a little box which he opened to reveal a dazzling ring full of sparkling diamonds.

"Will you marry me and be my wife forever?"

ALI

Secret sexual liaisons

BEFORE Leila and I got married, I had convinced myself that I would be able to restrain my sexual desires and direct them towards my wife. I had convinced myself that using up my sexual energy with my wife would be enough to extinguish the flames of my libido and would help me to be the faithful husband that I wanted to be, to keep my forbidden yearnings at bay.

I was determined to keep this promise to myself and to commit myself to respecting Leila's rights. I swore to myself I would do everything in my power to resist my urge to be with a man. I didn't object when Samir chose to keep his distance from me and go and work abroad. In fact, a week before my wedding, we went out to celebrate his new job with Royal Jordanian Airlines, and we said farewell forever on the night of the wedding. He acted like any other guest: he danced, sang, clapped, and ate supper like everyone else. He stood at my side when the news came about Salma committing suicide. And then he gave me a firm hug and a kiss on the cheek, and whispered farewell and good luck.

I missed Samir terribly for months, but I managed to keep myself together and get used to living with the pain of my memories. A breath of sadness at his departure hung over me and darkened my mood for months until I finally pulled myself together and accepted the reality, and started to get used to life without him. But though I triumphed over this grief and managed to endure the pain of my love for him, I ultimately failed to resist my sexual need for a man.

Is the torment of love easier to bear than the torment of the flesh that craves sexual satisfaction? I don't think so, but then maybe it varies from one person to the next and from one situation to the next. For me, both are painful. Love can only be satisfied by one person—the one you love—whereas with physical lust, while the one you love is the best person to quench your thirst, you can at least find satisfaction with someone else.

I got used to satisfying that urge by myself in the first few months of my marriage to Leila just as I did as teenager and at the times in my life when I didn't have a suitable sexual partner. I made up for my difficult sexual encounters with Leila by indulging in fantasy, picturing myself in the arms of other men. I started looking at gay porn sites and found myself getting drawn in, captivated by the lust that kept me pinned to the laptop screen for hours on end.

But my imagination got carried away. Those sites were a distraction that made me lose sight of my initial reason for using them, namely helping me to endure my marriage and my abstinence from gay sex, and to help me stay faithful to wife. Instead, they started to add fuel to my lust in a way that I didn't intend, and I started to become obsessed with the idea of meeting up with a man to satisfy my urges. I started browsing through men's profiles on gay dating sites. There were so many men just an email away! All of them looking for sex. Totally unabashed, they listed their sexual preferences and some uploaded photos and even videos of their private parts.

My profile was blank. I added a pseudonym and wrote just one line: 'Married man looking for secret sexual liaisons.' The invitations started rolling in from all kinds of men with nothing in common apart from their gender and their desire to have sex with other men. Many didn't stir the slightest interest in me, whereas some of them turned me on the second I saw their picture, prompting daydreams of me with them in an intimate embrace. I added some of the guys from the dating site to my chat app and started flirting with them in quite sexually charged conversations, which always got me really horny.

For a while I kept those liaisons confined to my online existence and cut things off if a guy insisted on meeting in real life. This went on for several months until I started to find myself being the one requesting that we meet up. The sex talk started to seem dull without the alluring possibility of meeting in person, and it was at a time when my relationship with Leila was taking a turn for the worse. She was developing an amazing ability to create problems out of nowhere. I badly needed a distraction in my life, a spark of excitement to lift me far away from Leila and our difficult day-to-day reality. I just wanted the occasional little adventure to bring me back home to Leila in a better mood and feeling calmer and more patient.

The excitement wasn't just from the physical meeting and the sex, but also from the suspense, as I waited for our rendezvous, imagining this unknown man and then recognising him in person. There was also an element of fear that added to the thrill. The risks were enormous, but the sneaking about in secret and keeping Leila in the dark all added to the buzz. That is, until that fateful day...

I suddenly had a bout of the runs one evening when I was in the middle of a particularly raunchy sex chat online. I rushed to the bathroom, thinking I had closed the screen and shut down the chat-room application. I was in such a rush that I didn't double check that I had exited the app properly and it didn't occur to me that the window might still be open. I certainly didn't imagine that Leila would be so bold as to invade my privacy. So I had no idea what was going on when I went back to my study to find Hassan crying and Leila unconscious on the floor.

I quickly took Hassan out and asked our neighbor to look after him while I tended to Leila. I immediately called for an ambulance and then went to fetch my cologne. I opened the bottle and wafted it under her nose, hoping to bring her round. I knelt beside her and put her head in my lap. I rocked her gently and kissed her forehead, begging her to wake up.

A few minutes later, she opened her eyes, not knowing where she was. She looked at me with a puzzled expression, trying to recall what had happened. And then her brow was knotted into a frown and her confused look turned to one of anger.

"Get away from me! Don't you dare touch me!" she yelled at me, pushing me away and screaming in my face. I tried to come closer to calm her down for fear she might faint again, but her fury flared up the closer I came. I had never seen her like this before. She seemed to be seized by a fit of madness, as though oblivious to what she was saying.

"You bastard!" she screamed at me. "You vile, dirty bastard!"

I still had no idea where on earth this sudden explosion had come from. I tried not to jump to any conclusions which might be wrong. Although I feared she might know something about my sexual liaisons, I wanted to hear it from her first, to work out how much she knew and how I should react. I tried to keep calm and ask her to explain why she was so mad at me, why she was cursing me like this. But I couldn't get through to her. Even when she stopped screaming, she was still crying inconsolably.

"Are you cheating on me with a guy?" she asked, finally. "Are you having gay sex? *Why?* Am I not good enough for you? Am I not pretty enough? Fine, but at least cheat on me with another woman, for God's sake! But a *man?*"

To start with, I didn't want to acknowledge what Leila was saying. I thought I would be able to deny it and convince her that it wasn't true. I tried to look surprised and shake my head with an expression that suggested I thought she was delirious. I asked her what had brought all this on, why these accusations out of the blue? I asked her if someone had been gossiping and telling her things about me that weren't true. I thought maybe one of the guys I'd met over the past few months might have carried out his threat of exposing me because I refused to give him money in exchange for sex. I was ready to refute it and give a different side to the story to convince Leila.

But she didn't give me the chance. She had seen proof with her own eyes: she had seen the sex chat online. She confronted me head on, and there was no way I could deny it. So instead I collapsed down in front of her and confessed. I don't know how I even managed to utter the words. I was choking as I spoke, terrified of the effect the truth would have on her, terrified of her anger and what it might mean for our relationship and our marriage. I was in floods of tears as the words spilled from my mouth. In a jumble of words, I begged for her forgiveness, trying to explain to her how much her I cared about her, how precious she was, and how deeply sorry I was to have hurt her like this.

I told her everything. I told her how I had succumbed to the social pressure to get married that had been as hard to bear for me as it was for her. I told her how badly I had always wanted children and a family to bring colour and joy to my life. I told her that I loved her and that I thought I would be able to give her the life she deserved. I told her that I thought I would be able to change my sexual inclinations and be faithful once we were married. I admitted to her that I had failed and told her how incredibly sorry I was to have deceived her and to have made her live this lie with me.

Now she possessed the full truth, and it was in her hands for her to deal with me as she saw fit. I deserved to be punished and she had every right to make me suffer. Once I'd said everything there was to say, I looked at her, my face full of apology. I wiped away my tears and waited for her to pass her sentence.

But her reaction was the last thing I expected. She got up and came over to me. She threw her arms around me and burst into tears.

PART EIGHT

LEILA

Curse that damn machine

IT'S so easy to judge others and make assumptions about their actions and their reactions to events in their lives. It's true that the grass is always greener on the other side: you don't know what something feels like until you're there yourself. And it's like fire and water: when you see them from afar, of course you can make out the shape and colour, but you don't feel the soft flow of the water or the harsh sting of the fire until you're up close.

I was no different. Whenever I heard about one of my female relatives being cheated on, I was always astonished at their ability to forgive their husbands and live with the injustice and the humiliation. How could they bear to stay married to them after being treated like that? I always assumed they must be pathetic or stupid to give their husbands a second chance.

But the world isn't like it's portrayed on TV and in the movies. We can never truly understand what it feels like to live through a disaster until it hurtles into our life like a hurricane, turning everything we cherish upside down. When my own world came crashing down, when I saw Ali's laptop screen that day, I felt so weak and utterly afraid. All I could think was, *Curse that damn machine!* It was on the computer screen that we lost Salma, and it was on the screen, too, that I lost my husband, the man I loved, and my whole world.

My mind simply couldn't endure the horror of what I saw, so I suppose I tried to switch it off, and immediately fainted from the shock. When I came round, in Ali's arms, I was hit once again by the horror of the reality that had taken over. I screamed like I had never screamed before. I needed to hear Ali deny it, to tell me I was mistaken, that it was just a hallucination, that my eyes were deceiving me.

So I was stunned by the shocking confession that suddenly filled his face with pain and remorse as the words emerged from within him. I heard him say awful things that I simply couldn't absorb, things which made me realise that the life I had lived the past three years was a lie, words that struck a line through everything I had thought was true.

I was living a lie. I was living a lie. I was living a lie.

This thought seized control of my mind as I heard Ali talking. I longed to hear something in his words that would reassure me that not everything in my life was a lie and that something remained as I knew it, that something at least would stay with me. The most essential thing was that Hassan was still real. The most painful thing was my feelings for Ali.

Although my heart was shattered with the shock of the truth, the greater impact was the pain I heard in Ali's voice and which was evident in the tears in his eyes. I've always been weak in the face of tears. My eyes well up the moment I see someone else crying. It's like my tears are desperate to show solidarity with a friend, to stand at their side like protestors declaring their solidarity with people in distress or under siege.

Men's tears are the worst. Maybe it's because I'm not used to seeing men cry, and perhaps because it's a rare sight it reflects the sincerity and strength of the emotion behind the tears. That was the first time I had seen Ali cry and, although my anger was as deep as my love for him, I was stunned when I found myself hugging him and bursting into tears.

He begged me to take my time to think it through and come to a decision as I saw fit. He said he wanted to make our marriage work and that he wanted Hassan to grow up with both his mother and father. He told me he would continue to carry out his duties as a husband and a father, but that he needed a little freedom. He couldn't suppress his sexual needs, he said, but he promised he would keep his meetings with other men to an absolute minimum, and that he would always maintain complete secrecy about his liaisons so it wouldn't affect our family or how other people saw us.

I asked him to try having therapy. And I asked him how he could do such a disgusting, hateful thing? A religious man like him? Who never missed a prayer and always observed the fasts—or was all that a lie, too? He tried to dispel my doubts, assuring me that his religious belief was sincere. He admitted that although he did believe within himself that what he did was *haram*, that it was wrong, he truly had tried to change himself and to resist, and had even tried psychotherapy, but to no avail. He said that the scientific articles he had read about psychology suggested that his sexual orientation, as he described it, was not a psychiatric illness, and there wasn't any way you could influence it or change it.

He told me all this and stressed that it was in my hands and that he was ready to do whatever I wanted, including us both going to a psychiatrist if I wanted confirmation. He was ready to do that for my sake, although, as he said, he had tried it before and felt he had been deceived and exploited. I did want to hear the opinion of a specialist myself, so we visited three different psychiatrists, and two of them said the same thing Ali had said: that his sexual orientation was perfectly natural and couldn't be cured. The third rejected that idea and gave us a lecture about religion and morality, and stressed how dangerous homosexuality was for society.

I was left feeling pretty confused about it all. As well as seeking the opinion of various doctors I also did my own reading in books and online. I found a tremendous amount of information and lots of heated discussions, and there was a definite contrast between the East and the West in terms of how people viewed it. Even among the psychological interpretations, what was prevalent in the West differed from what was widespread here.

I don't know why, if it was human weakness on my part, or whether the various strands of my reading started to coalesce and form a new consciousness within myself, but the more I thought about the different experiences and opinions of people who were in the same boat as Ali, the more I found myself—despite him having been unfaithful to me and deceiving me—sympathising with him and starting to understand his situation.

Are our ideas like our clothes? They seem to fit initially, but they become too small for us as our awareness about our surroundings grows, and then it's perhaps time to throw them off and replace them with new ways of thinking.

But just because I started to see Ali differently, it didn't detract from the disaster that had struck and the impossible situation I found myself in. Although all this inevitably implied an abrupt end to my sexual life, and therefore presumably the death of our marriage, I still found myself rejecting that as a foregone conclusion. Something inside me wanted to cling on to what remained of the life that I was used to.

I looked around me and weighed up the options I had. As far as I could see there were only two. I could find myself being labelled a divorcee, a status that carries even more stigma than being a spinster. It would mean social suicide and could have a disastrous psychological impact on Hassan and his social development. Or I could carry on my life as it was. As if nothing had happened. I could carry on in my role as a wife and a mother, and sacrifice my sexual needs for the sake of preserving the image we have in the community as a model family.

Should I go back to my father's house and accept all the social constraints that would limit my comings and goings even more than before I was married? Should I give up my image as an exemplary wife and mother, with all the admiration and respect it brings, and swap it for the image of a divorced woman who is viewed by everyone with either suspicion or pity? And as for my sexual life: how important was that, anyway, when compared to other aspects of my life?

But why should I sacrifice my sex life, when Ali refused to give up his? Were Ali and I just assuming I had to accept this blatant injustice because were both brought up in a society that shows no regard for a woman's sexual needs? Why should we accept that a man should be able to satisfy his needs and desires while denying this right to women? Even if a man's desires are deemed unacceptable by religion and by society, they still take priority over the desire felt by a woman.

Ali was aware of all this, and that's why he suggested I could be free to have another sexual partner if I did want to keep our marriage going. I was outraged. I found the suggestion highly offensive and contrary to all the moral values I was raised with. I would rather never have sex for the rest of my life than sleep with a man I wasn't married to.

But I started to realise that sometimes our hardships seem insignificant in comparison with the misfortunes of others. I saw that what had happened to me was nothing compared to my cousin Hiba who divorced her husband after two unbearable years of physical abuse. And I was surely better off than my cousin Abir who was forced to trawl hard-core porn sites for ways to turn her husband on when he threatened to take a second wife, because she wasn't, as he put it, fulfilling him sexually. And then there was our neighbor who discovered her husband was cheating on her with his secretary, and when she confronted him about it, he didn't deny it, but instead told her of his intention to marry her. In fact, was my husband cheating on me with a man perhaps better than him cheating on me with another woman? All I knew was that I had so much pain inside me. My heart felt crushed, and my life seemed like it had lost its meaning.

Was I supposed to go back to my father's house and yet carry on living at Ali's expense? I was furious with myself for having left my job and cutting myself off from a future career. I felt I'd lost my sense of who I was and how much it meant for me to excel and to stand out for my achievements. When I became a wife and a mother, I really did think that I had achieved everything I wanted from this world, but now the only thing I was sure of was that I desperately needed a job where I could succeed, which would give me back my independence and my self-confidence.

I found myself starting to entertain a refreshing new idea: I could go back to uni again. I was always so eager to learn, and it would be an opportunity for me to regain a bit of my confidence and my faith in myself as an independent person. It would push me to keep my mind active without impacting too much on the family.

Ali loved the idea. He encouraged me to try something new, so I chose gender studies, something that seemed unfamiliar at first, but which started to grow on me as I got into it and as it started to reflect different aspects of my life. The sexual discrimination which had haunted me through every stage of my life was embodied in every passage I read in the books on the reading list. Every word I read seemed to have a transparent thread linking it to the hurtful, misogynistic words imprinted in my memory.

I've always seen injustice as one of the worst things that exist in this world. Today I see it incarnated before my eyes in a worse form than ever. Not just because of Ali betraying me, but also because of the social system that has always felt like shackles around my ankles and which imprisoned me within a fictitious marriage. It is the same injustice that pushed the most precious person in my life, my dear sister Salma, to commit suicide out of fear of a dark future full of restrictions and taboos that would only increase as she got older.

And just as I used to have to battle against sexism and prove what I could do at school and university, I now felt the urge to stand up and defend women's rights more broadly. My lips could no longer suppress the volcano bubbling up inside me; my throat could no longer restrain the voice that needed to speak out.

I've resigned myself to my reality, but I've also started to direct that energy inside me towards standing up for other women. So after I finished my master's degree, I set up some support groups to enable women to help each other stand up to various forms of injustice. And shortly afterwards, that led to deciding to establish a national association that campaigns for an end to the social constraints that prevent full equality between the sexes.

This is how I filled that emotional and sexual void and

completely transformed my life. My work restored my confidence in myself and in my ability to make a change and help transform the lives of many other women, too. Ali remained my partner on paper, but with time he also became a true friend and companion. He shared with me both the charity work and the work of raising a young child, and everything we achieved was thanks to him, too. As far as everyone else was concerned, we were a normal family, you might even say the perfect family: the kind of ideal family that prompts admiration from others, and perhaps even a touch of envy.

Rana

Love suddenly appeared before me in its most glorious form

S O, two years went by and my father still wouldn't speak to me. I asked my mum every day if he would come to the phone. In the early days, I used to tell her about my life with Janty, the ups and downs of my pregnancy, the challenges of acclimatising to Sweden and the harsh winter. Every day I would tell her how much I missed my family, how homesick I was for our house, my room, her baking, and her hugs.

And then I would talk to her about the birth and about Sarah, the little angel who arrived to join our family. I would describe Sarah in every possible detail, including her every movement and the incredible changes she went through in the first few months of her life. I never tired of filming every single part of her body, and I'd send videos to my mother by email. Our phone calls would always end with me crying and asking about my father, and whether he'd forgiven me yet or not.

In the past few months, mum has begun to reassure me that his anger has softened, and that he has started letting her talk about me. She says he sometimes even shows interest in my news and wants to hear how I'm getting on.

I was surprised yesterday when she said that someone wanted to talk to me on the phone and wanted to hear my voice. A few seconds later I couldn't believe my ears when I recognised my dad's voice on the line. He spoke in a serious tone, tinged with sadness.

"Hello, baba," I heard him say. "How are you?"

I burst into tears as I was hit by a torrent of emotion. Oh, Dad, how I missed your voice!

My father was always there to support me, giving me a sense of pride and confidence. Although I was aware of the difficult position I had put him in, something inside me kept on believing in his love for me and that he would go to the ends of the earth to defend me and protect me. His silence and his avoidance of me hurt as much as my feeling of guilt about putting him in this position.

And now here he was, siding with his fatherly instinct. He was finally being true to the person I believed in, the man I once knew.

"Forgive me, darling."

I felt like Jesus Christ on the cross. That sentence hit me like a sharp stab, spilling my love like blood and reaffirming my trust in humanity. Love, the greatest of all our shackles and social imperatives, suddenly appeared before me in its most glorious form, in my father's voice. Honour may have distorted all other social values, elbowing its way to the front, but love remains present in our hearts, ready to light up our way and bring us back to our senses.

"No, don't say that, Dad," I said, unconsciously letting out a sob. "You're the one who should forgive me... please forgive me."

On the threshold of a reunion, all mistakes are forgotten. Neither of us cared any longer about the mistakes the other had committed. What was important was that our relationship as father and daughter proved to be stronger than everything else, stronger even than honour.

***

They came to visit us a month later, my father and mother, though not my brother. He still refuses to talk to me or acknowledge my existence, perhaps because he's still young and he feels he needs to prove himself and his macho credentials. He'll grow up and get over it with time. But it was wonderful that my mother and father could come and be with me finally, after two long years of separation.

I wished they could stay on with us indefinitely, but the lovely days we had together went by so quickly and, before I knew it, it was time for them to leave. Their visit left a deep impression on me and intensified my feeling of homesickness and nostalgia for Jordan. It also proved that we had turned the page on the past and that we had made a fresh start. It prompted me and Janty to start thinking seriously about returning home.

My parents weren't too keen on the idea as they were still afraid of the threat to us from our extended family. They insisted that I keep quiet about coming back and not tell anyone. My father decided to stand up in defiance of everyone and to tell his brothers that he had forgiven me and that he would not allow any of them to cause any trouble for me. He explained to them that I might have made a mistake, but I had made amends by marrying Janty in a Christian wedding ceremony.

And so we set off home, just as we had left in the first place. We left cautiously and we arrived home cautiously, as quietly and subtly as possible. We found an apartment close to Janty's family, far from the prying eyes of my extended family. We knew very well that our lives were still in danger: although the risk had abated somewhat, it had not gone away. We were also well aware of the dark past that we carried on our shoulders and how difficult it would be to live among people who—even if it's got nothing to do with them—are always ready to pounce on you and hurl moral judgements your way.

But things turned out a lot better than we imagined. Although I was saddened by some people's reactions and that some people kept their distance and avoided us, I also experienced more acceptance, love, and openness than I ever expected. Life showed me that the people of Jordan are inherently kind, contrary to the common perception portrayed by the media. Just like any other people, they are good-natured, open-minded, and sensitive.

Often I try to conceal my past, but with some people whose paths cross with mine I feel like opening up. As we get to know each other, I start to talk frankly about my life story. Though I'm always slightly wary of their reaction, time has taught me that honesty is the greatest virtue, and that people value the trust I place in them when I open up my heart to them. Perhaps that's why I find people tend to accept me with love and understanding, no matter how shocking my story.

Janty remains just as he has always been: my darling, my love, the one for whom I would sell the world, and who would sell the world for me.

Sometimes love is the greatest sacrifice as well as the greatest source of suffering. I don't regret the choices I made in the past. Love is a feeling you can't put a price on and my happiness might have been blown away by the wind long ago, had I not clung to it and fought for it.

I've come to see why Romeo and Juliet paid for their love with their lives. I thank the Lord that though my love cost me dear, he didn't make it cost me my life or the life of the one I love.

What worries me is Sarah's future and the impact our past might have on her, because people have long memories and there are people who would make children answerable for the actions of their parents. I pray that I will never be the cause of unhappiness for her, that I will never be a stone thrown at her in hatred.

I do everything I can to show my daughter how much I love her, and I am determined to arm her with confidence and knowledge. I hope to sow the seeds of love and freedom in her mind, and I always intend to remind her that she is the master of her own destiny, and that I'll always be there to support her, no matter what choices she makes in life.

ALI

We live for our children

I was stunned by Leila's decision to keep our marriage going and to keep the family together. It was a huge sacrifice on her part which I didn't expect at all. Although, as much as I was afraid of losing my family, part of me was prepared for that to happen and was even quite looking forward to reclaiming some of my freedom. But Leila sacrificed so much for me, and I had to make my sacrifices too, even if just for the sake of my son.

There has been—and indeed still is—plenty of male sex in my life, but the thing I have had to deal with and suppress is my need for love. This is was what bothers me and torments me whenever I realise I have feelings for one of the men I meet and that those feelings are mutual.

Passing flings always leave me with a psychological battle and great sadness. I'm tormented by a huge sense of guilt towards Leila. Here she was, altruistically putting her family first before her own feelings, and sacrificing both love and sex for the sake of Hassan. How could I, having already betrayed her, go on behaving like a selfish teenager, putting her whole world at risk?

I think we differ from Western societies in that we live for our children, while they live alongside their children.

We tend to go out of our way to compromise on our own happiness and needs for the sake of our children, while in the West they recognise that if their own needs are met, their children are more likely to be happy too. After all, can a child truly be content if he sees misery on his father's face? Can children grow up happy if their parents give them everything at the expense of their own happiness?

I suspect many of us don't appreciate the sacrifices our parents make when they raise us, and neither do we realise that those sacrifices are equal to the happiness they derive from their children. Or perhaps the happiness always outweighs the sacrifices no matter how great they are.

Leila found a way to direct her energies towards a greater goal and started to dedicate her life to a very worthy cause. I am so proud of her and so amazed and impressed by the tireless effort she has put into setting up her charity. She has been unstoppable. This strength seemed to grow within her that I had never seen before. It was as if she was born to fight this cause, that women's rights was her place in the sun to thrive. Women popped up out of nowhere like wild flowers in a field and Leila organised them into support groups according to their needs. She gave them succour in the form of the principles of equality and independence, and encouraged them to speak up and assert their rights.

Her passion for gender rights even grew to include lesbians, members of the transgender community, and sex workers. Her being married to me in no way limited her activities and her work. In fact, in fact the opposite may have been the case: perhaps our relationship was the spark that motivated her to devote her life to human-rights issues.

With her charity work, we have become one large family united by a sense of humanity. The spirit of the charity has spread like a delicate fragrance through our house. She has established a life of caring, of getting involved, a life filled with optimism and hope for a kinder future.

Sometimes life screws you up. It stuffs you into a corner and leaves you for dead. But it also endows you with an incredible ability to adapt and develop in a way that turns your weakness into strength, raising you from your cramped corner on to a regal throne. And so from our unusual situation, Leila and I have earned respect and admiration in our role at the forefront of the community.

HAYAT

I so wanted to be happy on my wedding day

EVEN knowing my father, I was surprised by how possessive he acted when he met John. It was as if he saw him as a rival he had to compete with. He didn't oppose me marrying John, who announced his intention to convert to Islam, but he also didn't leave a single stone unturned when it came to demonstrating that he was still my legal guardian and he was in charge.

He started interfering more in the last few weeks leading up to our wedding. He would bombard John with questions as if it was an interrogation. He seemed to be competing with him in trying to make me happy and comfortable, to the extent that a sense of fear started to creep into my heart that he might go back on his decision to allow us to marry. He kept looking at me with a sad expression and telling me how hard it was when I was far from home, and how worried he was about me traveling and living overseas. He seemed to be struggling with a wave of jealousy and the way he looked at us made me feel really uncomfortable. More than once he managed to seize on a moment when we were alone together to look at me with a mournful expression and apologise for what had happened.

"Forgive me, darling."

I was torn apart. His words filled me with searing pain, as though he were sprinkling salt on a wound that had not yet healed up. What kind of apology is that when I've lived my life torn between a child's longing for her father's embrace and a childlike terror of him at the same time? He was asking me to forgive him at a time when I no longer knew if I had any feelings left towards him at all, when there was no longer anything I could do to turn things around within me.

My father, whom I've always loved somehow, and whose compassion and affection I've always longed for, the father who raised me in a safe, secure home, was also the same person who tore that feeling of safety to shreds and crushed any sense of trust I had in anyone around me.

I was afraid I would let slip a moment of sympathy, or that a tender, loving hand would reach out from under the rubble of my memories. Perhaps it's the victim-abuser complex, or the hidden link between the torturer and his victim, but I did pity him. I pitied his grief and his remorse. I pitied his sick mind. What an awful feeling his remorse must be: the remorse you feel for hurting someone you love. In fact, is the torment of regret for the deed committed perhaps greater than the pain endured by the victim? How painful it must be to realise that in a moment of madness you crushed the person you held most dear, your own daughter? But perhaps it was precisely one of those moments of madness that made me think this way, and made me pity someone who did not deserve pity.

I had to try to avoid those moments and focus on the preparations for the wedding. I focused on the happiness of the occasion. I focused on feeling triumphant and being the centre of attention among my friends. *Here I am*, I thought; *I'm no different from any of them. Here I am, like the best of them: I too can be a bride. Like everyone else, I have the right to enjoy every minute of it.*

I was astonished to get a phone call from Leila a week before my wedding, just as I had surprised her the week before hers. I hadn't heard from her in over two years, since I tried to dissuade her from marrying Ali. And now here she was insisting that I see her. She wanted to apologise, she told me when we met, for not realising back then that I was telling the truth.

"Hayat," she said, blushing, "you are one of most sincere people I've ever known. Now I understand how difficult it must have been for you to know what to do. Forgive me, darling, I beg you."

It was plain to see how much she regretted not believing me at the time and how awful she must have felt when she realised it was true. She said that having called me a liar made it all the more painful when she did realise. She was fully aware of the pain of injustice, especially the cruel feeling of being pushed away when you're trying to do the right thing. It reminded me of the verse by the classical poet Tarafa Bin al-'Abd:

> *To be stabbed in the back by a loved one feels,*
> *More brutal than a blade of Indian steel.*

Little did she know that I'm quite used to being wronged by my loved ones and being stabbed by their steel daggers.

"I was so selfish that day, I was only thinking about myself. I thought I was the queen of the world, and that you must have a grudge against me because you were jealous. I couldn't bear to believe anything that threatened my dream and my excitement." She hugged me tightly, then burst into tears. "My happiness was all an illusion. I was punished for it the very day of my wedding when we lost Salma."

I suppressed my initial feeling of satisfaction when I saw the pain and remorse in Leila's face. I felt terrible for her, but also happy that she had come back into my life. I was gripped by a feeling of nostalgia for the past, as if our friendship was reborn after a long winter, putting down roots that were stronger and deeper than ever before. The pain of the past had branded our friendship with the indelible mark of love.

I told her about how I met John and how much I loved him, how happy he had made me since he came into my life. I also opened up to her that day, and for the first time in my life I found myself speaking about my father and my childhood, and the pain I had endured in secret. I told her about our wedding the following week and how I would love her to be there too and to share my happy day with me. She was silent for a while after hearing all that, and when she spoke it was hesitantly.

"Hayat, you were frank with me just before my wedding," she said, "and now I can't help but ask you: do you really love John, as you say, or are you looking for a way to escape? Doesn't the age difference bother you?"

What a hard question that was to answer! I could have quickly reassured her by insisting that I felt happy with John and I really did love him and was so excited about starting a new life with him, and that he loved me and treated me like a princess. But the truth was I did feel a few bubbles of doubt bobbing up and down inside me, and as she asked me, I was trying to stop them from floating up to the surface.

Am I trying to run away from reality? Have I in fact just convinced myself that I love John so I can escape from the cycle of horror that has always surrounded me? Am I ready to leave everything behind and start a new life in another world? Those whispers of doubt were the last thing I wanted to deal with just days before what was supposed to be the happiest day of my life!

I dismissed such thoughts, pushing them aside for our wedding and burying them just as I had buried every other image of the past. The only thing I wanted was to enjoy my special day—a day when all negative feelings are swept away by music and dancing, the day when all my loved ones would gather around me to celebrate.

My mum and dad were dressed in their finest as they greeted the guests, with my younger brothers at their side. Everyone was smiling: it was as if we were a happy family just like any other. Dad puffed himself up tall, towering over everyone and beaming with pride. Perhaps it was relief because this marriage would help whitewash over his past transgressions.

I, like any other Jordanian bride, was an innocent virgin in the eyes of the assembled guess. And he, like any other Jordanian father, was standing proudly before everyone, proud to have accomplished his mission in raising me and to be handing me over to my husband.

Did he even realise how long ago I lost my virginity?

He didn't dance, for custom dictates that a father never dances at his daughter's wedding—it wouldn't be seemly, after all, and that is the last thing he would want. He maintained his dignified standing in his guests' eyes, holding his head up high, having accomplished his task of passing his burden over to another man. My mother danced, bursting with happiness for me, but she was also tearful about seeing me go.

I couldn't keep up with all the different emotions that evening. None of it helped with trying to chase away memories which kept flitting through my mind like the slideshow John and I had put together to give the guests a flavour of our past lives. Every picture was loaded with memories and feelings I had suppressed all these years. One flashed by of me as a teenager standing next to my mum at Eid al-Adha, prompting a wave of pain deep inside, in a place I thought had long healed up.

Those awful teenage years are behind me, thank goodness, the years when I hated myself, when I hated my father and my mother. The days are behind me when I felt sure that my mother knew what my father was doing to me, but was turning a blind eye, leaving me at his whim so he would leave her alone. Maybe she hated him and his body as much as I did, so maybe she left me to endure him so that she didn't have to. On several occasions I was convinced that she must suspect something, but she was too weak and afraid of him to dare reveal it or confront the truth. She had left me alone all those years and now, on my wedding night, she was sad to see me go.

Trying to shake all those thoughts from my mind, I hugged her tight, there in the middle of the dance floor. I grabbed her hand with my right hand and with my left I grabbed the hand of John's mum, who had come all the way from the US to celebrate with us. I couldn't help wondering—whose was the best mum?

Leila and Rana came over to join the circle of women on the dance floor which then widened to include Ali, Samir, and Janty. Clapping to the beat, they all circled around me and John, who was struggling to keep step with the Arabic rhythm. I felt so happy to be there in the midst of all these people, these friends.

I looked at John at that moment and my heart was filled with joy, reassured to see in his face a picture of indescribable happiness. It made me feel like I was in safe hands, that finally the man in my life was a source of happiness, love, and safety. In his arms, I closed my eyes and let myself dream of a happy life that would make up for all these past years, those years that are well and truly behind me now.